"Let me help clean up," Mark said, swiping the dishrag from Hannah.

Warmth crept through her, making her want to smile, to stand near him and chat about the day while they worked side by side.

She shook the thought out of her head and busied herself putting away leftovers. The kids played in the next room, leaving Mark and her alone in the kitchen.

Enough.

"My turn." She tried to take back the dishcloth, and their hands tangled in the soapy water.

"I don't see how you do it all," he said.

"It was difficult in the beginning, but I'm getting used to it."

"Do you ever get lonely?"

"Most of the time I'm too busy to think about it. But sometimes, like on Valentine's Day, I wish for a knight in shining armor to shower me with flowers and jewels." Hannah laughed. She felt silly for admitting it. "Dumb, I know. But a girl can dream, can't she?"

"Not dumb at all. I have a few crazy dreams myself." Mark stared into her eyes for a moment before glancing away.

Books by Missy Tippens

Love Inspired

Her Unlikely Family
His Forever Love
A Forever Christmas
A Family for Faith
A House Full of Hope

MISSY TIPPENS

Born and raised in Kentucky, Missy met her very own hero when she headed off to grad school in Atlanta, Georgia. She promptly fell in love and hasn't left Georgia since. She and her pastor husband have been married twenty-plus years now, and have been blessed with three wonderful children and an assortment of pets. Nowadays, in addition to her writing, she teaches as an adjunct instructor at a local technical college.

Missy is thankful to God that she's been called to write stories of love and faith. After ten years of pursuing her dream of being published, she made her first sale of a full-length novel to the Love Inspired line. She still pinches herself to see if it really happened!

Missy would love to hear from readers through her website, www.missytippens.com, or by email at missytippens@aol.com. For those with no internet access, you can reach her c/o Love Inspired Books, 233 Broadway, Suite 1001, New York, NY 10279.

A House Full of Hope

Missy Tippens

Love Inspired

Recycling programs
for this product may
not exist in your area.

LOVE INSPIRED BOOKS

ISBN-13: 978-0-373-81605-7

A HOUSE FULL OF HOPE

Copyright © 2012 by Melissa L. Tippens

www.LoveInspiredBooks.com

Printed in U.S.A.

And now these three remain: faith, hope and love.
But the greatest of these is love.
—1 *Corinthians* 13:13

But because of his great love for us, God,
who is rich in mercy, made us alive with Christ
even when we were dead in transgressions—
it is by grace you have been saved.
—*Ephesians* 2:4–5

To my children:

Tyler—
my very own budding aerospace engineer
and hero in his own right.

Nick—future earth and ocean scientist
and soon-to-be Duke University graduate!

Michelle—future photographer/interior designer/
writer/mother/anything-you-want-to-be
(I'll adore you no matter what).

Mom is so very proud of all of you.

To God—
Who loves me generously and unconditionally.

Acknowledgments:

A big thank you to Matthew McWhorter
and Amy Hagin for research help—
especially Amy for answering my many
text messages. To Janet Dean for quick reads and
spot-on feedback. To Lindi Peterson for friendship
and moral support. And to Janet and Lindi for
helping me figure out the ending!

Thanks to my wonderful agent, Natasha Kern,
for believing in me.

Thanks to Emily Rodmell, Rachel Burkot and
all the fabulous people at Love Inspired Books
for their hard work and dedication.

Chapter One

Asking for forgiveness from a man like Redd Ryker was sure to backfire.

But Mark Ryker had returned to Corinthia, Georgia, to apologize to his father anyway. Because God had hit him with conviction far more compelling than any fear of Redd's reaction.

As Mark traveled through the overarching trees along the long, winding driveway, he recalled the peace it used to give him as a boy. But for several years before he moved away, even the calm, light-speckled green tunnel offered no relief from his grief. From his guilt.

He braked and stared at the house that had sheltered Rykers for generations. He couldn't believe the poor condition of his dad's home. *Home.* Not quite a fitting term for the house during Mark's teenage years, yet he did have some good memories here.

Memories from before his twin brother, Matt, died.

The overgrown front walk led to a house, once a cheery yellow, which now sat sallow and peeling. The roof needed replacing. When he stepped onto the porch, he found a shutter tilted at an angle, and a screen door that didn't sit flush. The pair of old rocking chairs, the one place his parents used to seem happy, were mildewed and caked with bird droppings. Why had the old man let the house go? Finances? Lack of interest after Mark's mother had died?

He blocked the pain that thoughts of his mom dredged up, took a deep, fortifying breath and knocked.

A few seconds later, footsteps approached from the yard. He turned and stood face-to-face with his father. He hadn't seen the man in fifteen years, and every one of those years was now etched in his craggy face.

Stooped and rail-thin, the man who once intimidated Mark looked far older than his sixty-five years. But the hard golden eyes that perfectly matched Mark's hadn't changed a bit. They revealed his anger even while registering shock.

The hope Mark had cautiously nurtured over the past few weeks as he'd prayed and prepared for this moment died a quick death, shoving his stomach to his knees.

His father opened his mouth to say something,

but then he closed it into a tightly drawn frown, shutting off the words.

The first move would be Mark's. "Hi, Dad."

A flash of emotion flickered in the man's eyes, but then vanished as if snuffed out. "What are *you* doing here?"

If Mark said he'd found the Lord and had felt led to come, his dad would probably laugh him out of town, or worse, accuse him of sacrilege. "Can I come in for a minute?"

Redd's eyes flickered to the front door. "I don't see why you'd show up here in your highfalutin clothes and suddenly need to set foot inside a house you abandoned years ago." He turned to walk away.

"Dad, please…"

The man Mark remembered as hard and unfeeling paused, his shoulders hunched. Almost as if turning Mark away was difficult.

Mark knew he had to act fast. "I'd like to apologize. For so many things. To—" The words lodged in his throat. Words that were difficult. How could he explain his fierce independence, that he'd stayed away from everyone he cared about, determined to achieve success, to make them proud before he returned? "I need to ask your forgiveness for all the trouble I caused. And for leaving like I did."

Redd's gaze locked onto Mark's and narrowed.

"Why *now?*" The question oozed suspicion as much as venom.

Okay, Lord. Here's my opportunity. "Because I've changed. God has forgiven me, and I'm trying to live a new life."

For the first time, his dad drew up to his full height and squared his shoulders. "How dare you? Your mother was the finest Christian woman that ever lived. And now you come back here and dishonor her memory, spouting religious mumbo jumbo? What do you *really* want?"

Though Redd's reaction was no more than Mark deserved, hurt seeped into his bones, weighing down his limbs. Why had he bothered? "Nothing. I just wanted to say I'm sorry."

His dad avoided eye contact and looked somewhere over Mark's shoulder. "I don't want no apologies from you. I'm ashamed of you. There's no fixin' that."

The words sliced through him. Though he'd expected this visit to be tough, he hadn't expected total rejection. "I won't keep you, then."

Once his dad stomped away and disappeared into the garage, his escape hampered by a pronounced limp, grief Mark hadn't anticipated seized him by the throat. He'd caused so much pain. Apologies couldn't repair the damage.

The old feeling of hopelessness reared its ugly head. A feeling he'd thought he'd put behind him years ago when he'd pulled himself out of the pit of drunkenness and despair. Or rather, when God had used the New Hope Mission to pull him out of the pit—well before Mark had acknowledged the turnaround of his life as God's work. He'd taken years to grow up to the point he was ready to turn back to God, to invite Him back into his life.

And then it had taken many months before Mark had felt God's leading to come home and face his past.

But as his dad said, there was "no fixin'" to be done here in Corinthia. *Lord, I tried.*

He trudged to his rental car and cranked up the air conditioner, wishing he'd formed a backup plan. He'd come all the way from Seattle; he shouldn't give up after one try. If he stayed around for the weekend, he could find out why the house was in such bad shape.

But he also had to try one more time to talk with his dad. Maybe if he did, he would at least find a measure of peace—if not redemption.

Hannah Hughes loved the new office that came with her recent promotion to bank branch manager. A large wooden desk faced the door, and she'd hung her children's original artwork on the walls surrounding her. A nice, cozy work space. And though the job demanded more of her time and energy, she appreciated the pay raise that had enabled her to rent a bigger house for her kids. She'd be up to speed on her new duties soon enough.

She turned to her computer, hoping to knock out some of the time-sensitive reports so she'd get off early enough to cook a decent dinner for her kids.

A man's voice carried across the lobby and in through her open door. His cultured, soothing tone made Hannah relax in her chair as she tried to decipher what he was saying to Amy, their new part-time teller. But something in Amy's voice put Hannah's senses on alert.

As she rolled her chair back, a man in sunglasses holding a briefcase stopped in her doorway while Amy, wide-eyed and wringing her hands, peeked around from behind him. "Um, this gentleman is looking for Mr. Jay. I thought maybe you could help him."

Poor Amy. She was new enough that she must've thought the man was a threat.

"Thank you, Amy." The teller walked away, and Hannah said, "Mr. Jay retired last month. Is there something I can do for you?"

As the man looked around, she cataloged him: six feet tall, wavy dark blond hair, expensive navy sports coat...and maybe a niggling of something familiar?

"Possibly," he said. "Do you have a moment?"

Hannah calmly stood. "I'm sorry, sir, but could you please remove your sunglasses?"

He slowly reached for them, as if he didn't realize he had them on. "Oh, I'm sorry." He tucked them in the pocket of his finely made jacket and looked up.

Those eyes. Such a unique light golden color... cat eyes—the Ryker eyes. Ryker eyes?

She sucked in a breath. *Mark.*

"May I speak with you privately for a moment—" he glanced at her nameplate "—Ms. Hughes?"

Could this really be the town's infamous bad boy? He hadn't been around since he dropped out of high school and ran off—leaving a swath of devastation in his wake. She clenched her fists and forced a pleasant, neutral expression. "Have a seat, Mr. Ryker."

The unusual yellow eyes narrowed. "You know my name?"

"I recognized the family resemblance." She motioned toward a chair opposite her desk and sat.

"You're correct. My name is Mark Ryker. I'm originally from Corinthia but left Georgia years ago. You must know my father, Redd."

Yes, she did. She'd looked at those same golden eyes nearly every day. The eyes of her landlord.

Hannah tried to maintain her professional face. Not easy when this man, who'd thrown her childhood into chaos, was sitting across the desk. "What can I do for you, Mr. Ryker?"

"Jason Jay is an old family friend. I had hoped to talk with him about my father's account. To make sure his finances are in order."

The man sat there calmly, his striking, larger-than-life presence smacking of arrogance. Though he looked like a successful businessman, that couldn't change the fact he was the reckless punk who had led Hannah's sister, Sydney, down a destructive path.

She pushed away the memories and checked the churning knot of anger to get to the task at hand.

"May I ask why?" Though his intentions weren't any of her business, she felt protective of her kind landlord.

Just as Mark opened his mouth to answer, Police Chief Gabe Reynolds stepped into her office, his dark hair windblown. "Oh, I'm sorry. I didn't know you were busy." He eyed her customer.

"Hello, Chief Reynolds," she said. "We'll be through soon. Can you come back in a bit?"

Mark didn't turn around. He sat still, as if he wished Gabe would go away.

Seconds ticked by as Gabe eyed the back of Mark's head. "I see the rental car out front. You new to town or just visiting?" His amiable smile faltered the longer Mark sat without speaking.

Then Mark sighed, although Hannah didn't actually hear a sound. It was more like he simply deflated. "Yes, Officer. I'm here on bank business," he said, while turning his head slightly toward Gabe to acknowledge the man's presence without actually showing his face.

He's trying to hide his identity.

Gabe wasn't having any of that. He walked around to the side of her desk to face Mark head-on, and Hannah wanted to cheer.

The weasel was forced to stand and look Gabe in the eye. "Hello, Gabe."

Gabe's eyes narrowed, and he shook his head as if he couldn't believe who he was seeing. "Mark? Mark Ryker?"

Mark offered his hand. "Yes, in the flesh."

Gabe didn't hesitate to shake his hand, but he didn't offer a smile and a clap on the back like he might do for someone else who'd returned after so many years. "So, what brings you home?"

Mark glanced at Hannah. "Banking business."

"Well, I'll let you two get back to it. I hope you'll stop by and see your dad while you're here." She heard the challenge in Gabe's seemingly innocent comment.

"I already have. But I'd like to keep my business at the bank private. I'd appreciate it if you don't mention it to anyone—especially my father." Mark's manner bordered on threatening.

Or maybe desperation disguised as threat?

"Okay. As long as you'll promise me you're not here to hurt Redd."

Pain flashed in Mark's eyes, but his expression didn't change. "Of course I'm not here to hurt him."

Gabe seemed to accept Mark's word and left her office with a nod and a wave.

Once he was seated again, Mark pinned Hannah with his feline stare. "I need to know you'll keep my visit confidential."

Drawn to those scary yet beautiful eyes, like she had been years ago, she couldn't have looked away if she tried. "As long as you mean no harm."

That same pain flashed once again before he looked away. "I noticed my father's house in a state of disrepair and wanted to inquire about possible financial troubles."

Hannah's face burned. Redd had told her he was renting out the place because he didn't want to live alone in such a big home. She'd tried to overlook the condition of the house, assuming he'd been too busy running his hardware store to handle repairs. But now she had to wonder about Redd's motivation.

Had he moved into the garage apartment so he could earn money by renting the main house? "I'm afraid I can't share any information about your father's accounts unless your name is on them."

"Mr. Jay has done so in the past. I used to check in with him about once a year to make sure my father didn't need any financial help."

"And what about his well-being? Did you inquire about that, too?" she sniped before she could stop herself. She held up her hand to hold off an answer. She didn't even want to know. Didn't want to spend another minute dealing with this man. "Again, I'm not authorized to divulge account information."

Mark's jaw twitched as if he were grinding his teeth back and forth. "Thank you for your time."

She took his outstretched hand and forced herself to look into his face—his too-handsome face, a scar near the left eyebrow the only thing marring its perfection. She hated to continue the conversation but needed to know his plans so she could make sure to avoid him.

"Will you be staying with your dad while you're visiting?"

She thought for a minute that he might laugh, but then she realized it was a grimace. "No. I guess I'll need you to point me to a hotel."

From the look of him, he liked nice things. He might not appreciate their little motel over by the lake. "The Cardinal Motel is still here. Or the

Gunters opened a new B and B not far from your dad's house."

"Thank you, Ms. Hughes. I'll try the B and B." He stared at her a moment. "You look familiar. Is Hughes your married name?"

"Yes." Part of her wanted to ignore the questions and hurry out of her office. But another part wanted to tell him her maiden name. To see if he even remembered ruining her sister's life.

She chose the latter. "I'm Hannah *Williams* Hughes."

He sucked in a breath, then quickly closed his mouth.

Oh, yes. He definitely remembered. Not that his remembering could change a thing for Sydney.

Stunned, Mark stared at Hannah Williams. He couldn't believe God had led him back to Corinthia to make amends, then tossed a Williams into the mix the moment he hit town.

Dealing with Hannah would make his job that much more difficult. "Good to see you again, Hannah." A rote reply, even though he'd rather be anywhere but talking to Sydney's sister.

She didn't return the sentiment. She simply brushed past him and walked out of her office. "I'll see you to the door."

He followed as she marched across the high-ceilinged lobby, the click of her high heels echoing off all the marble. She was trim, but the boxy skirt and fitted jacket couldn't hide her curvy figure. How could he have not recognized her vivid green eyes?

She'd been a pesky middle-schooler when he'd dated Sydney. Had worn dark-framed glasses back then and had been serious, studious. She used to stare at him—until he'd finally asked her why. She'd blushed and claimed she wasn't staring. After that, she didn't hang around often. Acted scared of him.

Which was smart. All girls should have stayed away from him at the time.

At the front of the lobby, she held the door open for him. Her expression, cool and closed, said his actions had not been forgiven or forgotten over the past fifteen years. Apparently, his father wasn't the only one holding a grudge. He would need to make amends with the Williams family, as well. A daunting task.

But obviously, God expected it.

"The B and B is a couple of miles out, on the left, heading to your dad's house. Is there anything else you need?" Hannah asked from her post as bank bouncer, her tone dismissive.

If only he could just thank her and head out the door, straight back to Seattle. *You can do this with God's help.* "No, thanks."

Hannah, as pretty as she was, glared at him, her anger evident. "Enjoy the visit with your dad."

He gave her a smile that used every last ounce of energy, then slipped his sunglasses back into place.

An ache tore through his chest as he concealed his Ryker eyes. It would be best to remain anonymous since everyone else in town would probably feel the same way Hannah did. The way his dad did.

Redd would never welcome him back. Would never forgive him for all the hurt he'd caused when he left town. *Lord, help me to make amends while I'm here. And if it's not too much to ask, please enable those I've hurt to forgive me.*

Even if Mark *could* somehow prove God had changed him, that he'd grown up to make something of his life, he knew he was after the impossible. Because the fact still remained: Mark was responsible for his twin brother's death. His dad would never forgive him for that.

Chapter Two

That evening, Hannah drove to pick up her four children at her mother's duplex apartment not far from the bank. Their daily stampede to the front door to greet her never failed to lighten the stress of the day. Even the stress of facing Mark Ryker. *They're such a joy, Lord. Thank You.*

Donna eyed her from head to toe, as if taking inventory. "Hello, Hannah. Rough day?"

Obviously, she looked harried. "A little."

Without a hair out of place, Donna directed the kids to gather their belongings, which sat neatly packed by the front door. Always a bundle of energy, she didn't look like a woman who'd watched a house full of kids for nine hours. Even her hazel eyes seemed bright, not tired. The woman was amazing. Only the streaks of silver at her temples and scattered through her brown hair gave away the fact that she was a grandmother.

"Come on, kids. I imagine you're hungry."

Donna smoothed Tony's hair. "You know good and well their nana wouldn't let them leave hungry."

"We had a snack," the twins called in unison.

She thanked her mother for babysitting and hurried them to the car. She made sure all four were buckled in her minivan and then she drove toward home.

"There's our old house," Becca said, same as she did every day, as they approached the apartment complex they'd called home for the past seven years.

Hannah looked in the rearview mirror and discovered Becca, with her dark pigtails and pink-framed glasses, staring out the window. "Yes. Do you miss it?"

"I do," Tony said. Her child who didn't like change. Who hadn't wanted to move so far from his nana.

"Not me," Becca said. "I like having my own room."

She slowed as they passed. So many memories at that apartment, good and bad…

Memories of Anthony and her moving in when Becca was a toddler and Tony was a baby. Tony taking his first steps across the kitchen floor. The surprise of another pregnancy. Bringing home the twins to a too-small apartment. Struggling through those early days with no sleep and tons of bottles and diapers. Trying to make sure Tony and Becca got enough attention while taking care of newborns. Watching her husband, Anthony, drag in the door each evening, worn-out from working overtime to support their expanding family.

Anthony getting more and more tired. To the point he could hardly work. Then those life-altering words from her husband's mouth: "I have cancer."

That simple sentence reverberated through her mind as if he'd uttered it just yesterday. Hannah stifled a sob and beat back the grief that clawed and left her raw inside. Grief that could suck her under its dark, smothering weight if she let it. *No time right now. Too much to do.*

She closed the door on the painful memories and forced herself to look ahead. She had four beautiful children who were her world. And she had finally provided them the spacious house she and Anthony had always wanted for them.

Lots of space to run and play. Five bedrooms—one each. A huge kitchen with a table big enough to hold everyone plus friends and family. A room with lots of shelf space, the perfect library for nine-year-old Becca and her precious books. A barn and woods for seven-year-old Tony to explore. And a brand-new swing set she'd bought on layaway for six-year-old Emily and Eric.

She turned to look at four smiling faces in the back of the van. Sweet faces that never failed to lift her spirits. Their unconditional love was the only thing that had kept her going the past two years, that had given her the strength to start this new phase of their lives. "Well, our new home is working out well."

Becca pushed her glasses higher up on her nose, her big brown eyes wide with wonder. "I wish Nana would babysit us at our new house. There's so much new territory to explore, so much to show her."

Since Becca's nose was always in a book, particularly of the Nancy Drew mystery variety, Hannah had no doubt the old farmhouse had opened up a whole new world for her daughter. But Hannah's mother refused to set foot on Ryker property. "We'll see."

As she drove away from downtown Corinthia, the courthouse and storefronts shrinking in her rearview mirror, Hannah imagined she could breathe more deeply. Along the ten-minute drive, homes grew farther apart, and the landscape changed to pastures dotted with cows or horses and the occasional farmhouse.

When she reached Redd Ryker's mailbox, she turned onto their property and glanced at the dashboard clock. Mark's visit, and the fact that he'd left her stewing, had put her behind all day long.

"Since it's so late, how about I make frozen pizza for dinner?"

Squeals and clapping hands rattled her brain as she wound along the dirt-and-gravel road for about a hundred yards. Trees arched over the drive from each side, forming a canopy dappled with the evening sunlight. The tranquility even managed to quiet the kids.

"I love this part," Tony whispered.

They entered the clearing, and the house came into sight. The squeals and clapping began anew.

"Can I play outside?" Emily begged.

"Me, too?" Eric added as he unbuckled and tried to climb over Emily to get out first. He could never let Emily do something before he did.

"For about a half hour." Hannah pointed to the left side of the house toward the garage apartment where Redd lived. "Y'all play in the side yard or out back in case Mr. Redd drives up. Be sure to stay out of the way."

"Okay, Mommy!" Emily yelled as the four escaped from the van to play under the huge live oak tree towering over the freestanding two-story garage. Hannah unlocked the front door, stepped inside and nearly tripped over boxes that still needed unpacking.

Two weeks since they moved, and she'd barely made a dent in the number of boxes. But with her job and the kids home for the summer, she could hardly find time to cook and do the laundry. Unpacking had to be done in bits and snatches.

She went to turn on the oven to preheat, then plopped down on a box marked *Hughes—kitchen.*

Though she was thrilled to have the house, disappointment nibbled at her joy. She had hoped to build her dream home, a haven for her and the kids, and to finally experience the security of owning a home. But once the medical bills and funeral expenses had been paid, the insurance money was nearly gone. Anthony had made the mistake of procrastinating on increasing his policy once the children were born.

We're young and healthy, he'd said. *We need the money for groceries.*

And, foolishly, she hadn't insisted he rectify the situation. Now, all she'd been able to afford was a larger rental property. Home ownership would have to come later.

She opened the box she'd been sitting on and dug to find the round baking sheet. After washing it, she pulled the pizza out of the freezer and popped it into the oven.

The kitchen was slowly looking homier. At least now they didn't have to squeeze into a three-bedroom apartment, and once school started in the fall, they wouldn't be stepping all over each other as they got ready for work and school in the mornings. Even if the Ryker house didn't belong to them, it was still theirs for the time being.

As long as Mark didn't cause a problem.

The front door banged open, and Becca barreled into the room, winded. "Can we let Blue out of his pen?"

She smiled at her precious daughter, who'd begged for a pet for the past three years. Redd's dog, a sweet and endlessly patient black Labrador retriever, had been almost as big a draw as the house. "You sure can."

As Becca zipped back outside with an echoing whoop of joy, worry crept over Hannah. What if Mark had come home to stake a claim? She looked around a room where Mark and his brother, Matt, would have eaten their meals with friends and family.

What if Mark suddenly had an interest in the family home?

Hannah knew she would do whatever she had to do to keep her kids happy.

Since Hannah had thwarted Mark's plan to check into his dad's financial state, on Saturday morning he decided to return to the house and do a closer inspection. To estimate the cost of needed repairs.

He'd assumed Redd would be at the hardware store, but an unfamiliar green minivan sat parked out front. The truck he'd seen the day before was gone. He should probably knock before walking the property. In case his dad was there. And if he was...

Well, Mark would try once again to apologize.

This time, he looked more closely as he inspected the dirty front porch that fronted three sides of the old home. When he reached the far corner, he caught himself grabbing for the cobweb-covered broom as if he were still ten years old. Sweeping the porch had been his and Matt's job—a chore they'd deemed too girly.

He smiled at the memory, yet being on their old stomping grounds intensified the emptiness that never quite left him.

Matt, who'd suffered mild brain damage at their birth, hadn't been as strong and healthy as Mark. Mark had always tried to include him, though. But one day when they were fifteen, and their dad shooed them from the hardware store, Mark talked Matt into going fishing on the lake. Into taking out their dad's boat, knowing good and well they weren't supposed to go alone...knowing Matt couldn't swim.

As he turned away from the broom and faced the front door, he doubted his sanity. Only a glutton for punishment would return to this house again. *We are more than conquerors through Him who loved us,* he reminded himself, a Bible verse he had clung to for years.

He raised his fist to knock, but something tugged on his pant leg.

"Hi, Mister." A little boy about five or six years old stared up at him with big brown eyes. "Are you looking for Mommy?"

After a glance around the porch and yard, he squatted down to the child's level. "No. I'm looking for my, uh…" *daddy?* "…father."

All business, the boy crossed his arms and seemed to ponder the situation. "You look kinda old to be lost."

Trying to match the boy's expression, Mark stifled a laugh. But then sobered when he realized how close to home the boy had hit. "Actually, this is my house. My dad lives here."

The kid shook his head. "You really *are* lost. 'Cause this is my new house."

Laughter sounded somewhere off to the side of the house. Then three children appeared around the corner, chattering. One by one, they stopped talking when they saw Mark.

Only the youngest girl approached and tromped up the steps. "Who are you?"

"He's lost," the first boy said, as if imparting the juiciest of secrets.

"Lost?" The oldest girl hurried up the steps and scrutinized Mark. "How exciting." Large brown eyes that matched the youngest boy's widened. She peered at him from behind pink, sparkly plastic-rimmed glasses. "I can help. I'm good at solving mysteries."

A bush swished as the last child—a boy somewhere between the oldest and younger two in age—kicked around the overgrown shrubbery, ignoring the investigation on the porch.

Mark turned back to the others. "Actually, I'm looking for my dad, Redd Ryker. He lives here. And you are…?"

"My children."

Mark turned and found Hannah Hughes behind the screen door. Inside his family home. She looked even less friendly than yesterday.

"See, I told you this was my house," the youngest boy said.

Hannah stepped outside, and as the door swung open, Mark caught a glimpse of boxes in the entryway. As if someone was moving.

He pointed to the boxes. "What's going on?"

"Kids, go wash up. There's a snack on the table."

Once they'd scampered into the house, Hannah turned back to him. "We're renting from your father."

Incredulous, he sputtered, "That can't be. My dad would never rent this place. It belonged to his grandfather." And was Mark's home, even if he hadn't set foot in it for years.

A sudden longing to be close to his mom again made it difficult to speak. He wanted to go inside, see what had become of his old bedroom. Of his spot at the kitchen table. Of his mother's things.

Hannah looked away, almost guiltily. "Apparently, he's decided he doesn't need such a big house and prefers to live in the garage apartment."

The garage? No matter how badly Mark had wronged this woman's family, he couldn't let her run all over *his* family. "Look at this place. It's run-down. My guess is you took advantage of his financial difficulties."

There it was again—a flash of guilt. "We simply responded to an ad in the newspaper."

He took a step closer and stared into her eyes. They were a beautiful, pure green and couldn't hide a thing. "Now I understand why you wouldn't give me information about Dad's finances at the bank yesterday."

He had to give her credit. She didn't back down. No, she actually leaned in closer. "I told you. I don't have authorization to divulge information on your father's accounts."

"Accounts, plural? Maybe including a line of credit?"

Her face revealed a flicker of something he took as confirmation before she turned away. "I need to go check on the kids."

"I see you're not settled yet. I suggest you and

your husband wait to unpack. Before I leave town, I'd like to know that all Dad's finances are in order and he's back in his home."

"I have a signed contract that says we're staying."

"I guess we'll see about that." As he strode to the garage, he promised himself he'd get to the bottom of the situation. If his dad was in the bind he suspected, then Mark had to make sure he was financially secure. Redd might refuse to speak to him, but surely he wouldn't refuse help. Mark would park himself in the garage if he had to, until his dad listened to reason.

He banged on the upstairs apartment door. But of course, there was no answer. Redd would be at the hardware store, probably all day.

He plopped down on the top of the steep outside stairs and leaned his forearms on his knees. He'd come home to apologize. That was it. To say he was sorry, have his dad pronounce forgiveness, and then head back to Seattle.

And now he'd found the man in a mess.

Well, Mark had nothing to do with the situation, so he *could* just run by the store and apologize one more time. Then be on his way.

But a nudge in his gut—the same one he'd trusted when he'd come here in the first place— told him he needed to see this through.

He opened his cell phone to two measly bars of

service and managed a staticky call to his assistant. He informed her of his change of plans.

In several years, Redd would be facing retirement. He should be able to sell his store and live in comfort—not in some apartment over the garage.

It might take Mark two or three days, but he would not leave town until he knew his dad was okay financially and settled back in his home. He owed him that much.

"I found him first."

"Uh-uh. We all found him together."

Hannah stepped between the twins, their riotous wavy hair adding to the sense of perpetual energy and motion that surrounded them.

"No one found Mark. He wasn't even lost. He was here to see Mr. Redd." She pointed both children toward their new bedrooms. "Now, no more arguing. I switched the schedule to have this Saturday off work so we could do some more unpacking."

Becca whooped from her room across the upstairs hallway, the sound bouncing off the hardwood floors and high ceilings. The only drawback to a larger, older house was how noise carried. And boy, did her family produce noise.

"I'll help each of you arrange your room the way you want it," Hannah said. "Eric, you first."

Eric huffed and pointed at Emily. "No fair. She'll get to play longer while I have to do chores."

"No more arguing. Get to work."

Tony stuck his head out his door. "When's Nana going to come see my new room?"

The child loved his grandmother, even with her faults—one of which was holding grudges. She was furious Hannah had moved into a house owned by *those Rykers*. All these years later, Donna refused to associate with Redd, even though he'd had nothing to do with his son's behavior.

"I don't know, sweetie. I'll be sure to invite her again, though."

Tony, named for his father, was the only one of the four with Hannah's green eyes. He was also the most sensitive. Hannah worried that her mom's refusal to come around would end up hurting him.

Of course, Mark showing up would not help one bit. Maybe Hannah could invite Nana out for the following week—well after Mark headed back to whatever rock he'd climbed out from under.

Those green eyes peeked around the door again. "Will you call her now?"

She knelt down in front of him and gently caressed his face. "Of course. Now, go figure out where you want to store your rock collection."

As he hurried to obey, she went downstairs to

call her mother from the phone in the kitchen, in case they ended up arguing.

Donna Williams picked up on the fourth ring. "Terrible timing, Hannah. I'm trying to get—" she grunted "—a pound cake into the oven." A thump like an oven door closing rattled over the phone. "Of course, if I wasn't on the bereavement committee at church, I wouldn't be doing this. But how could I say no when Ann called me directly with a request for one of my pound cakes?"

If Hannah just sat quietly, she suspected her mother could carry on a whole conversation by herself. Someday, she might test the theory. "So who's the cake for?"

"The Smith family. Maude died." The sound of water running blasted in the background. "And you can imagine how it burns me up to have to do something nice for that no-good daughter of hers. Frederica tormented you in second grade. You almost had to change schools. But, well, your daddy refused to move and instead taught you how to fight."

Yes, her mother still held a grudge against a second-grader who was now thirty years old. Hannah nearly laughed at the memory and made a mental note to give her dad, now remarried and living in Colorado, a call. She and her dad had often made her mother furious.

"Well, I survived. And speaking of moving…"

Banging of dishes continued. "No. I will not babysit out there."

"Come on, Mom. It's been two weeks, and the kids are dying to show you around."

"Why couldn't you just buy a nice little house in town? Or if you had to move out there to the boondocks, why not rent from someone else? Anyone but *those Rykers.*"

Hannah shook her head. Donna had always said the name with disdain. And she never used their first names. She lumped father and son together and deemed them both bad news.

Of course, Mark Ryker *had* turned their world upside down when he started dating Sydney. He'd had a reputation for being wild, and when Sydney began coming in at night with alcohol on her breath, their mom had tried her best to end the relationship.

But by then, Sydney was in love. Or so she had claimed. Hannah had always suspected she enjoyed hanging around a guy who was fun and easygoing like their dad—and not a bit like Mom.

"Mom, I'm not going to debate my decision with you. But I would like to invite you for dinner next week. Tony keeps asking when you'll come see his bedroom."

She harrumphed. "Well, you're not going to catch me setting foot on those Rykers' property.

Tell Tony he's welcome to come here anytime he wants to see his nana."

Don't say it, Hannah. Be calm. One Mississippi. Two Mississippi. Three Mississippi...

"Hannah, are you still there?"

"Yes." But she might have to bite her tongue off. *Four Mississippi. Five Mississippi.* She took a calming breath. "Please come out here one day next week to watch the kids. Redd will be at work. You won't run into him."

"Hannah, I warned you when you first looked at that house. You're just going to have to bring them to my house on your way to the bank each day. And snap some photos of Tony's room."

Once Donna Williams made up her mind, no one could reason with her. Hannah should be grateful she had free child care with a loving family member. But she did worry about her mother's attitude rubbing off on them.

"I guess I have no other choice."

"I'm sorry. But I will stand firm. Now, I'll see you at church tomorrow."

Yes, as much as she'd love to take another day to finish unpacking and get settled, she didn't want to miss the service.

Of course, if Mark had his way, she should keep the last of their belongings boxed up. He might, at that very moment, be talking his dad into forcing Hannah and her children out.

She gripped her aching stomach—a two-year-long side effect of chronic worry since Anthony's death. Worry about letting her children down. About not providing well enough on her own—emotionally or financially. What if one of the kids got injured or seriously ill? Or needed braces? What if *she* got injured or seriously ill, or lost her job? Or if a landlord decided to kick them out?

All the more reason to stick to her plan to eventually own a home. She wouldn't have to be at the mercy of a landlord. At the mercy of someone else to repair the property—or not. At the mercy of some man who could pop into town after fifteen years to try to ruin the life of another Williams sister.

But home ownership was years down the road. For now, she needed *this* house that she and the kids had grown to love. If Mark thought she would give it up without a fight, he was sadly mistaken.

Chapter Three

After a Saturday-afternoon attempt—and failure—to speak with Redd, Mark knew it was sunglasses-off time. No matter what happened with his relationship with his father, he had to let the town of Corinthia know that Mark Ryker was a changed man. And that he owed that change to the grace of God.

So on Sunday morning, he put away the sunglasses and donned the one suit he'd packed—more out of habit than because he thought he'd need it. He drove his rental car to the small church his mom had dragged Mark and Matt to when they were children.

Growing up, their dad had worked all the time and their mother had taken charge of raising the kids and seeing to their religious upbringing. Of course, Matt, the sweet, obedient child, had gone to church willingly. Mark had been another story.

He hoped his mother was looking down from heaven, seeing that her insistence and persistence had given him a foundation to fall back on years later, after his life fell apart. After he hit rock bottom and realized he could either die, or he could ask for help to climb out from under the guilt, anger and self-destructive behavior.

As the church came into sight, the thought of how far he'd come nearly overwhelmed him. He blinked back tears and, for probably the thousandth time, thanked God he hadn't gotten addicted to the alcohol he'd used to numb the pain. And that he'd hit bottom while at the New Hope Mission. With God's help, the staff and volunteers at the shelter had saved Mark's life.

The white steeple of the Corinthia Church loomed bright and welcoming. Mark parked and approached the old redbrick building. As he walked in the door, the organist struck up the hymn "Amazing Grace."

How appropriate. He had to smile at God's sense of humor. With that smile locked in place, he searched for familiar faces.

Of course, the first person he saw was Hannah with her four children. And another woman beside her who—

He stopped in his tracks, his heart dropping to the pit of his stomach. The woman was Hannah's mother, Donna Williams.

Hannah didn't look up. She was busy whispering—fussing over the two youngest kids. As he forced himself to continue down the aisle, he vaguely noted neither husband had attended. He would need to make time to speak with Donna, to apologize to her, as well. Maybe after the service.

As if Donna were a bloodhound smelling trouble, she looked right at him. It took her about two heartbeats to recognize him, but then her eyes flared wide. She froze in place, staring, her eyes lasering fury his direction. Her face reddened, and he feared she might explode with a torrent of words. Words she'd probably wanted to say to him years ago.

He moved on, hoping to avert a scene with Donna. When he glanced to the right, old Mr. Jay from the bank gave a polite nod. Then Mark spotted his dad up front in what used to be his mom's favorite spot, next to the organ. *So he has come around and now attends church.* This eased some of Mark's fears, and he started down the aisle toward Redd.

But about halfway, he stopped. What was he thinking? This was not the setting to approach his dad again. He would embarrass him. So he turned to the back to find a seat.

A dumb move that meant he had to face everyone he'd passed.

Gabe Reynolds, who'd gone to high school with

Mark, sat with a teenage girl and a woman Mark didn't recognize. The woman, pretty, pregnant and apparently his wife, smiled kindly. Gabe merely nodded.

Two rows farther, Miss Ann Sealy, one of his favorite people from Corinthia, sat with a young man who looked familiar. Maybe her grandson. She waved but had a blank look, as if trying to place him. He'd thought of all the people in town, she would've been the one to give him a profuse welcome.

His chest tightened as he realized how few people would even know him now. And of those who did, how they might view him with distrust.

Shame scalded Mark's face as he searched for the closest available seat. As he was sitting, he heard a commotion—Donna yanking her purse off the pew and stomping toward the door. Right before she exited, she glared at him.

After the door banged closed, he couldn't help but look at Hannah. She stared after her mother, mouth covered, eyes wide. When she turned to him, her hand dropped and eyes narrowed. Her scowl said she blamed him for the outburst. He could imagine her thoughts. *How dare you darken the doors of our church?*

Well, the Williamses had spoken. Mark figured others might also. Probably wouldn't matter that he was a new creature in Christ. How could the people of Corinthia ever see beyond the reckless boy who'd caused his brother's death, hurt Sydney Williams and then skipped town?

He tried to focus on the service, but couldn't get beyond the fact he was an outsider in his own hometown and might never be able to make amends. Yet God's Word and the music penetrated the worry. He eventually relaxed into the pew, felt God's peace wash over him. This was where God wanted him. He wouldn't give up.

After the service, Mark strode toward the front to catch his dad before he left. When Mark reached the end of the pew, he waited for Redd to look up, to ask him to sit so they could talk. Who was he kidding? His dad raised his chin and stared straight ahead.

May as well have slapped up a sign that said Not Welcome Here. Still, he had to take a chance. "I'm glad you're attending church, Dad. Mom would be pleased."

Redd grabbed the pew in front of him for support as he stood. Then he looked at Mark with utter scorn. "Your mother and I worshipped together here for years. But then, you wouldn't know that, would you?" He limped away, his squared shoulders a shield against his wayward son.

The jab hurt. Physical pain knifed Mark's chest. No, he wouldn't have known that. And he would regret it the rest of his life. Would regret that he hadn't come home sooner. That he hadn't come before his mom died.

He rubbed his chest, trying to ease the pressure. *Don't go there. Think of the future.*

Of course, he had no idea how to approach his father again in that future. Maybe the pastor could help. While Mark waited for the crowd to thin, he shook a few hands, drawing encouragement.

Miss Ann approached with a grin on her face. "Welcome home, Mark." She'd aged over the years, but her sky-blue eyes and extreme Southern drawl hadn't changed a bit. "You caught me by surprise this morning. Didn't recognize you at first."

"Thanks, Miss Ann. It's good to be here." An exaggeration. But it *was* nice to be following God's lead for a change.

"If you don't have plans for lunch, please join me and my grandson, Daniel." She pointed across the room at the man who'd been sitting with her. Then she puffed out her chest proudly. "He came to visit me this weekend and to meet with Pastor Phil. He's graduating from seminary soon."

"I wish him well." Touched by her kind invitation, he considered it briefly. But he had business to attend to. "I'd love to have lunch, but I need to speak with the pastor myself."

"Oh, you'll like Phil. He's been here a few years

and is a good counselor." She suddenly reached out and hugged him. "You take care, now. Your mama would be so happy to see you at church."

He closed his eyes and breathed in the scent of the same sweet perfume his mom had always worn—White Shoulders. Sudden tears stung the back of his eyes. He pulled away, cleared his throat. "Thanks, Miss Ann." He waved and hurried outside. No use in letting memories get him all choked up. No time for regrets, for worrying about something he couldn't change.

"Good to have you with us today." The pastor, who looked to be in his late forties with graying temples and a few smile lines around his eyes, stood alone on the church steps wiping perspiration from his brow with a handkerchief. He tucked it in his pocket and held out his hand. "I'm Phil Hartley."

"Nice to meet you, Reverend Hartley. I'm Mark Ryker."

"Oh, I see the likeness to Redd." Kind eyes encouraged Mark to speak up. It was as if the pastor could tell he'd been hanging around. "Please call me Phil."

"Thanks, Phil. Do you have a minute?"

"Sure. Let's get out of this hot sun and go to my office." He led the way through the sanctuary and along a hallway decorated with kids' artwork, all centered on the theme of Jonah and the big fish.

Apparently, the church still held vacation Bible school in the summer.

A sudden memory of arguing with his mother about helping with Bible school made him cringe. He'd told her he and Matt would rather work with their dad at the hardware store than with those wild kids.

She'd seemed hurt but had relented.

If only he'd known then what that rebellion would cost. If only he'd known how a rickety fishing boat capsizing in a pathetically small lake could change his family forever.

"Have a seat." Phil gestured to a grouping of three chairs set up in the corner of the room, obviously for meetings or counseling sessions.

"I won't keep you long. But I need a favor." He proceeded to tell Phil a little about his family background.

"You had a twin who died?" Phil's head tilted as if he was confused. Apparently, no one had ever told him the story.

Mark nodded. "It was my fault. I took him fishing, the two of us alone, knowing he couldn't swim. He died of complications from the near-drowning."

Pain filled Phil's eyes, and it caused an echoing pain in Mark. "Oh, man. I'm sorry."

He hadn't talked about this in years. Had to force words that didn't want to come. "My parents tried not to blame me. But I knew they did. And I buried the pain with alcohol. With rebellion. And unfortunately, dragged Sydney Williams into it."

"So that's the reason for Donna Williams's animosity toward Redd?"

With a wince, he confirmed it. "We started dating, and her family wasn't happy about it. I admit I'd fallen into a bad group of friends. Tried to pull her away from them when I saw she had a drinking problem. But it was too late."

"So what happened?"

"I ran. Just wanted to escape it all. Took off and didn't look back for years." By the time he tried to make contact, his mother had died. Too little, too late. The story of his life.

His old life.

Mark forced the corners of his mouth upward. "But I'm in a better place now. Found God again. And felt led to come home to make amends."

"Did you and your parents ever make peace?"

"No. Now Mom is gone. Dad won't speak to me. And—" He snapped his mouth shut before he broke down and embarrassed himself.

With fingers steepled under his chin, Phil nodded. "So you've tried to apologize to your dad?"

"Yes. I'm here because I need your help in reaching him."

Phil leaned back in his chair and crossed his

ankles. "I know Redd's a stubborn man, but I think he'll come around."

Mark's dad had always been stubborn. Stubbornly driven to build his hardware business. Stubbornly driven to punish Mark for Matt's death. "In case he doesn't, I want to at least help him financially. Did you know he's renting out his house to the Hughes family?"

"Yes. Also heard he's in a bit of a financial pinch. His store has had a rough time since the mega home-improvement store opened up not twenty miles from here."

Oh, man. He hadn't heard that news. "I'd like to make a deposit to his checking account. But I'm afraid Hannah Hughes will balk. She seems protective of him and…well…she doesn't think much of me."

"I don't know how I can help. We've already tried to give him assistance after his hip surgery, and he was offended." Phil shook his head. "Yet Redd's continued to donate funds to our youth program even as he's struggled."

Out of nowhere, Mark's throat constricted. It seemed he didn't know his dad at all anymore. Had God changed Redd, too?

"Stubborn, proud man." Mark stood and walked across the office to stare at a painting on the wall—more to distract himself than to admire the art. "If I give you cash, could you take it to the bank, tell Hannah you've received an anonymous donation and ask her to deposit it into his checking account?"

"No harm in trying."

The tension that had invaded Mark's shoulders the moment he'd approached his dad that morning eased away on a big exhaled breath. He turned back to face the pastor. "Thanks, Phil."

"This is generous of you, you know. I hope your dad realizes the man you've become."

Phil might think the gift was generous, but Mark owed his dad so much more. If all went well tomorrow, maybe he could set up an arrangement with Phil. A way to continue helping.

But would Redd accept the help if he found out Mark was the donor?

"Okay, I'm it. You better hide really well," Hannah called to her children Sunday after lunch as they squealed and scattered around the grassy front yard. She covered her eyes and started counting slowly.

The past couple of years, Hannah had only wanted two things. A bigger home for her kids— *check*—and the certainty that each of her children felt important and special.

But being a single working mom made that difficult. She struggled to make time for each one. Had dropped her volunteer position with the church youth group. Made Sundays family time.

"Don't peek," Tony called from somewhere behind her.

"Nine and a half. Ten! Ready or not, here I come." She opened her eyes just as Emily's head disappeared behind the rocking chair on the porch.

She grinned as she started rattling bushes and jumping behind trees. "Where is everyone?"

A giggle sounded at the side of the house. Within five minutes, she had found everyone, saving Emily for last.

Redd, who'd started closing Hometown Hardware on Sundays a few years earlier, gave a wave as he lumbered across the yard, his uneven gait making him rock side to side. His graying hair had once been dark blond like Mark's. And he'd probably been as handsome as his son in his younger days. But his wife's death six years ago had aged him. Deep wrinkles formed brackets around his mouth and frown lines between his eyes. The smile that lit his face when he saw the kids gave Hannah an inkling of what he'd looked like years before.

When Emily spotted him, she squealed and ran to hug him, dark hair flying in the wind. Eric followed closely and grabbed on to Redd's other leg. He hobbled across the yard, pulling giggling kids along with him. "Well, now, I seem to feel a bit heavy today. Must've eaten too much lunch."

Becca, in her standard pink T-shirt and denim shorts, grabbed her belly and doubled over, laughing. "Mr. Redd is so silly."

Tony, usually reserved, actually smiled. "He's teasing, Becca."

Her children loved Redd. And the man seemed to enjoy them, as well. In the beginning, she hadn't been too sure about their extremely close neighbor relationship. With the Ryker-Williams family history, she'd worried how he might feel about them being there. But from the beginning, he'd been solicitous, almost as if he still felt guilty for his son's actions.

Admittedly, she'd felt awkward at first. But she'd come around to the fact that Redd had been as hurt by Mark as her family had.

"Okay, you two. Don't hurt his hip. Let go of Mr. Redd so we can talk."

The twins pouted—for about five seconds. Then they raced off, calling Becca and Tony to come play another round of hide-and-seek.

Redd looked off into the distance, but his eyes didn't seem to focus on anything in particular. "I guess you've seen that Mark has returned to town."

Her stomach dropped at the mention of his

name. What if Mark had talked him into moving back in the family home? "Yes."

"I'd rather him not know I'm renting out the house, if there's any way around it."

"I'm afraid he came by yesterday."

He ran a hand over his chin, rasping against whiskers, looking troubled.

She gently touched his arm. "Are you okay?"

His chin rose as he watched the kids. "I'm fine." Then he looked into her eyes. "You?"

He tried to act cool on the outside, yet he had to be a mess on the inside. Meanwhile she stewed, worried and angry. "I'm okay. Shocked, but okay."

"Still can't figure out what he's doing here. Says he wanted to come apologize. But now he's hanging around."

Yes, it was unnerving, to say the least. And she felt sure he'd stayed to try to uproot her and the kids so his dad could move back into the house.

"He seems to be concerned that you're in the garage apartment." She wrapped her arms around her waist and watched him closely for his response.

He shook his head and huffed. "I'm fine over there. Don't worry about me."

Yes, but could Mark change his mind? "Well, I guess we can hope Mark's motives are pure."

Redd gave a snort but didn't comment further.

"I sure hope your sister doesn't find out he's back, even if it is just for a visit."

Goodness. Hannah had thought so much about her own situation with the kids and the house that she hadn't considered Sydney hearing about Mark being in town. "Yeah, me, too. She's still got a few more weeks in rehab."

Regret crawled across Redd's ragged features, drawing his mouth into a frown. He shook his head and plodded toward the garage, hands in his pockets, head down. As if carrying a huge weight. He stopped partway across the yard.

"I know the kids in the youth group miss you, but you made a good choice to spend Sundays with your little ones. They grow up too fast." Regret tinged his voice, and his pain jabbed her heart.

"You're right," she said, wishing she could say something more, something to comfort him.

He'd lost one son. And, really, the other, as well.

Now Mark was here trying to butt into his dad's life. The man might end up hurt all over again.

"Mom, I'm hungry," Tony called. "Is it time to eat yet?"

"Not yet, sweetie. But why don't you come inside and help me decide what to cook?"

Maybe if she finished unpacking, she wouldn't feel so unsettled, so worried about losing the

house. She would finish the last boxes that night,
even if she had to stay up to the wee hours.

Mark had the money in hand by noon on
Monday. When he arrived at the church, he
climbed out of the air-conditioned car. The muggy
afternoon air nearly sucked the breath out of him.
He'd forgotten how miserable it could get in early
June in Georgia.

Carrying an envelope of cash left him unsettled.
After years of living on the streets, he'd become
hyperalert. Cautious. Now he caught himself
glancing around, waiting for someone to jump
him.

He laughed it off and flagged down Phil as he
spotted him walking through the parking lot.

"Oh, hi, Mark. Is that the money for your dad?"

"It is."

Phil nodded toward the bank, which sat across
from the old brick courthouse with its newly refurbished white cupola. "Come on, walk part of
the way with me."

As they crossed the street, Mark said, "Did a
little research at the courthouse this morning. Dad
owes back taxes. This will cover that debt, plus
the larger home repairs." He handed over the envelope.

A flash of concern drew Phil's brows together.
"You know, Mark, I'm all for doing good. But

I hope Redd won't be angry when he discovers the deposit."

"Surely an anonymous donation will save his pride."

"We'll see soon enough." He gave Mark's shoulder a reassuring squeeze. "I'll have the receipt anytime you want to come pick it up." He nodded toward Faith's Coffee Time Café. "Miss Ann Sealy often spends her mornings over there with her Bible, visiting with friends…if you think you could use a friendly face."

As the pastor walked inside the bank, Mark decided Phil was very insightful. He did need a cup of coffee and a friendly face even more.

Movement flickered in his peripheral vision as he turned toward the coffee shop.

A little dark-haired girl stood on the sidewalk, craning her neck back, looking up at him. "Hello."

"You're Hannah's daughter."

She pushed her pink glasses higher up her nose, and stared at him with earnest brown eyes. "Yes. And you're the man who was lost."

He bit back a grin. No point in trying to convince her otherwise. "I guess I am." He forced a serious look on his face. "So what are you doing today?"

"I'm bored, so I'm walking to the library." Her pigtails swung in her face as she took off a backpack, unzipped it and pulled out a card. With a wide grin, she proudly held it up for him to see. "I have my own library card."

"Impressive."

She stuffed it back inside. "Where are you going?"

"To get coffee. Are you with your mom?" He glanced around, hoping Hannah was with the girl so she wouldn't find out about the deposit.

"No, I'm staying at my nana's, and she let me play outside." She crossed her arms and squinched up her nose. "I should probably ask her if I can go to the library."

"Yes, I imagine she'd be worried if she can't find you."

She sighed as if very disappointed to have to delay her visit to check out books. "I guess you're right. Bye, Mister, uh…"

"Mark. Just call me Mark."

A shy smile lit her studious face and made her bright eyes sparkle. "I'm Becca." She ran toward the church, crossed the street at the corner and then ran toward a group of older redbrick duplexes. She disappeared between two buildings. He assumed her grandmother—Donna—lived nearby.

Becca didn't seem to have noticed Mark walking with Phil. But he still didn't like the idea of Hannah's daughter seeing him near the bank. The last thing he needed was for Hannah to find out where the money had come from and tell Redd.

"Becca, please put down your book while we're eating." Hannah had managed to prepare a dinner of spaghetti and salad, though she never had located the box of kitchen supplies that held her colander. Dinner had also been delayed by her mother's half-hour rant about her fury over Mark's return.

As if Donna storming out of the church hadn't been indication enough.

"This spaghetti is watery," Becca said as she stuck a bookmark in the novel. "I wonder why."

"No mystery there. I can't locate the box with my pasta strainer."

Becca made a check mark in the air with her finger. "Aha! Problem solved."

Hannah smiled at her daughter. "So what are you reading?"

"Do we have to hear about one of her stories agaaain?" Eric whined through a mouth covered in tomato sauce.

"That's okay, Becca. I want to hear," Emily said, but then followed the sweet remark with a punch to her brother's arm.

Ignoring the whole exchange, Tony-the-bottom-less-pit, with his tousled brown hair and squeaky-clean face, bent over his plate, totally focused on shoveling in the pile of plain noodles he'd insisted on that night.

Though parenting by herself left her drained sometimes, Hannah wouldn't trade a moment spent with her children. "Let's all be nice. Becca, you can tell us about your new book. Then it's Tony's turn to talk. Then Eric's, then Emily's."

Becca's face lit with a smile as she pushed up her glasses and jumped right in with a complete plot summary. Then after she finished, with a dribble of spaghetti sauce on her chin, she added, "Oh, and I met Mark today. You know, the man who was lost? He and Pastor Phil were walking downtown while I was going to the library." She looked up to see if her story had attracted their attention.

Normally, Becca's asides wouldn't faze Hannah, but this one grabbed her by the throat. Phil had deposited a large anonymous donation into Redd Ryker's account that day. So Becca's information could mean Mark was the donor. It would make perfect sense.

"So did Mark say what he was doing with Pastor Phil?"

"Nope. He just asked if I was with you. And told me his name."

Goodness. She certainly hoped Donna hadn't made a scene. "So did Nana talk to him, too?"

"Um…well…" Her face turned red as she stared into her plate. "Nana didn't know where I was."

"Rebecca Lyn Hughes, what were you doing running around the square by yourself? And why didn't your grandmother tell me?"

She blinked her big brown eyes. "Well, I didn't think about asking. I was bored and started to go to the library. And then when Pastor Phil went into the bank, I stopped to talk to Mark." She broke from her hurried explanation long enough to gasp for a breath. "And I didn't think about asking Nana until Mark said I should. So I went back to the house to ask her if I could go to the library, and she took me. And I got my new book."

"Well, young lady, I'm afraid you're going to lose some of your freedom the rest of this week for breaking the rules. You can't play outside alone until Saturday."

Becca stared at her novel, as if wondering whether the unauthorized first trip to the library had been worth it. "Maybe I can do some reading at Nana's house."

"Certainly. No more wandering off."

They finished their meal, and after putting Becca in charge of the younger kids with instructions to unpack the last of their toys, she ran next door to Redd's apartment.

When he answered the door, he smiled. "What

a nice surprise. Come in." A table behind him had a plate and glass on it.

"I'm sorry to disturb your dinner. But I was wondering if you could possibly watch the kids for about thirty minutes while I…uh, run to town?" To see what his son had been up to. "After you eat, of course."

"Well, I reckon that'd be okay."

"You'll be fine. They're occupied with unpacking the last box of toys." She'd never been so pushy in her life, and her face burned hot now. But she had to find out what Mark was up to. If Redd had enough money, he might boot her family out of his house—if not now, then possibly at the end of the one-year contract, before she could afford to buy or build. She knew good and well she'd never find another rental house big enough that would fit her budget.

"I'm nearly finished. I'll be there in five minutes."

The poor man. She hated to hit him up for child care just because he was close by, but desperation necessitated it. Now she needed to hurry home to change clothes.

Change clothes?

Disgusted with herself for even worrying about it, she marched across the yard and told the kids the plan. Once Redd arrived, she sent them back to organizing their rooms, gave him her cell-phone number and then left.

Remaining stealthy was difficult in a small town. But she did her best to cruise by the B and B and check license plates without alarming the owners or guests.

Luckily, she found Mark's rental car parked out front. Of course, now she had to go inside and ask for him. Mr. and Mrs. Gunter knew everyone in town—including Hannah's mother. If Donna found out her daughter had come around to visit Mark Ryker, she would throw a fit. Or worse, do something irrational to punish Hannah.

She plowed ahead, intent on telling the man to quit meddling in his father's affairs and to go away. Helping Redd was one thing. But sneaking around, using money to manipulate him to do something he claimed he didn't want to do—like moving back into the house—was a different matter.

A sign on the front door of the old Victorian home said to enter and ring the bell on the desk. She followed the directions, then waited. Every creak made her jump. Still, no one came.

She knew there were four guest rooms. She could start knocking.

No. Too awkward. So she tapped the little silver bell again, louder this time. Still no response.

Instead of heading toward the guest rooms, she first searched the living areas. When she reached the dining room, she heard voices outside. She peeked through the screen door at the back porch and found Mark sitting on an oversize rocking chair, holding a coffee mug. He and two other guests chatted with the Gunters.

Evening social hour.

Fighting the temptation to flee, she squared her shoulders. She would not waste putting herself through that awkward request for babysitting by chickening out.

She pushed the door open. "Hello?"

Though she tried her best to smile and look at the owners, her gaze automatically darted to Mark, whose rocking motion stilled the moment he spotted her.

"Oh, Hannah, dear," Mrs. Gunter said from the chair beside Mark, in her thick German accent. An energetic seventy-year-old, she always wore cotton dresses covered with an apron…and knee-high stockings, the tops of which showed just below the hemline. "Come join us for cookies and coffee."

"Thanks, but I can't. I stopped by to talk with Mr. Ryker for a moment."

"Oooh?" Mrs. Gunter said, with a hopeful lilt on the end of the word.

Mark hopped up, leaving his chair to rock back and forth without him in it. "What can I do for you, Mrs. Hughes?" Though concern drew his brows downward, his voice sounded perfectly calm and…well, perfect.

How could he infuriate her so, even in that smooth tone of voice? And where had his Georgia accent gone anyway? Had he purposefully hidden it? Was he ashamed of his past?

He should be ashamed of his past, accent or not. "I need to speak to you about something—privately."

"You talk in the garden." Mrs. Gunter stood and shooed them down the back steps. She pointed toward a path that led into a garden surrounded by holly hedges.

The sun was heading below the horizon as Mark followed her farther along the path dotted with pink-and-yellow lantana, pots of geraniums, beds of petunias. At the last event she'd attended at the Gunters', a bridal shower, she'd thought the garden lovely, peaceful. But now, with the crescendo of frog calls, the oppressive, flower-scented air and closeness of Mark as he trailed behind her, right on her heels, the shrubbery closed in, smothering her.

At the first bench, she stopped and turned to him. "I know you donated the money for your dad."

"And how could you have come to that conclusion?"

He was calm and cool and totally irritating.

And those eyes…a woman could lose herself in those eyes.

She sat on the rough stone bench, mainly to get away from him. "Becca saw you outside the bank today."

He sighed as he sat next to her. "I was afraid of that. I really want to keep this anonymous. So please don't tell my father."

"You're afraid he'll reject the donation if he finds out it's from you?" As soon as the words left her mouth and she saw the hurt on his face, she regretted her question.

"I'm sure he'll reject it. He wants nothing to do with me—which I understand. But I don't want him to struggle when I'm able to help."

Pity tried to worm its way into her heart, but she stood firm. One time, many years ago, she would have fallen for his spiel, for his generosity. At one time, she would have thought him attractive.

But this man had ruined Sydney's reputation, started her on the road to alcoholism and then, when he realized what he'd done, vanished. She would not feel sorry for him.

"I don't plan to tell your father. The deposit is simply bank business as far as I'm concerned. But if you try to make my family move before we're ready, then I may have to reconsider."

He raised his brows with what appeared to be

humor. "Does your husband know you're here threatening me?"

A flash of pain shot through her. Though it had been two years since his death, hearing someone say *your husband* still hurt. "My husband passed away. I'm simply taking care of my family the best I can."

"I didn't know. I'm sorry for your loss." Genuine regret drew his brows back down from their teasing height and made him frown. Then he looked away.

If he'd had half a care for the people of his hometown, he would have known about Anthony's death. The tree frogs seemed to lapse as awkward silence settled around them.

"So how long do you plan to live in Dad's house?" he asked.

"Two to three years. I hope to buy or build as soon as possible."

He seemed to consider whether he could tolerate his dad living in the garage for a few years. She wished she felt better about it herself. She'd been dealing with guilt since she'd watched Redd move out of the only home he'd ever known, watched him climb those steep garage stairs several times a day. She clung to the fact he'd said he was tired of rattling around that big old house, hoping it wasn't strictly a financial decision. Now she couldn't help but wonder if Redd had been truthful.

Mark stood and casually rested his hands in the pockets of his khaki pants, almost as if he'd rehearsed the genteel country-club look. "The house needs a lot of repairs. Maybe I could stick around and help."

"So where did you get all this money to help your dad?" she blurted as she stood to face him.

A crooked smile raised one corner of his mouth, but no humor reached his eyes. "So you don't think I could have earned it?"

Instead of stating the obvious, she gave him a look that conveyed her doubt.

"A project I started in grad school grew into a successful business. I've been blessed financially."

Could she believe anything he said? "So tell me the name of this company."

"You won't recognize it, because our biggest contract is with the military. We've developed unmanned aerial vehicles."

"Like spy planes or something?"

He stared into her eyes, his sparkling in the last rays of sunlight. "I promise you it's all legitimate. I hope you'll believe me."

Grad school? Unmanned aerial vehicles? His tone—and those mesmerizing golden eyes—made her want to believe him. But she resisted his pull and snapped herself back to the problem at hand. "I don't know why I, Sydney Williams's sister, should believe a word you say."

"I'm a changed man, Hannah. Thanks to God."

Chills ran up her arms at his earnestness, at his conviction. But she wouldn't be duped. "That's nice."

"I'm serious. I'm here because I felt God leading me to come and make amends. And I guess that means I should apologize to your sister, as well."

An apology? Could mere words fix the past? Could they *fix* Sydney now?

Rage she'd held in for years simmered to the surface, trying to spew. She forced herself to speak in a calm voice, even as she wanted to get in his face and yell. "You know, after you left, my sister's world fell apart. She stayed mixed up in that horrible crowd you ran with. Alcohol gave way to drugs. She flunked out of school. Got sent to juvie, then rehab."

His earnest conviction turned to a look of disbelief. "I—I had no idea."

Hannah was on a roll, and it felt good to let out the pent-up anger, especially at the man who caused it. She jabbed a finger in his chest, wanting him to know he'd destroyed all their lives. "My world fell apart, too. The strain destroyed my parents' marriage. Their divorce—and a second round of rehab for Sydney—ruined us financially. Mom and I lost the house." Her words wobbled against her will.

She'd been a sad, confused teenager, longing

for a time before Sydney's addiction, a time when she, too, had mattered. But the house had been the worst part for Hannah—losing the only home she'd ever known. Living briefly in a homeless shelter. Moving to an apartment. Changing schools. Losing friends.

Mark couldn't run away this time. No, now he had to stand there and face the truth about what he'd done. She stared into his beautiful eyes to see if her revelation had affected him.

He hung his head, shaking it, staring at the ground. When he looked up, a sheen of tears reflected the moonlight in his eyes. She recognized anguish when she saw it.

Good. I hope he suffers a little of the pain I suffered.

He reached for her, then snatched his hand back. "I'm sorry. Is there anything I can do?"

A sob heaved from deep inside, but she tamped it down. "Even if you wanted to apologize to Sydney, you can't. She's in her fourth round of rehab." She turned to walk away but stopped. Tears burned her eyes as she stared at the blurry ground, then lifted her gaze to his.

"You can't just make a donation to fix that, now, can you?"

As Hannah walked away, a wave of nausea hit Mark full force. He sank to the bench and closed his eyes, head hanging, hands dangling over his knees. *Why, Lord? Did You bring me home for this? Not to apologize, but to see the destruction I left behind?*

The look on Hannah's face. Grief. Hurt. Anger that had been eating away at her for all these years.

He swallowed hard against the sorrow. Against the renewed guilt. No wonder Redd was still ashamed of him.

Lord, please show me what to do.

Sydney, such a fun-loving teenager, now in rehab for the fourth time. Hannah, losing her father, her way of life, her home.

All his fault.

Mark had no idea what, but he had to do something to repair the damage he'd caused the Williams family.

Avoiding the Gunters and other guests, he wound around to the side entrance and went to his room. He called his assistant to extend his vacation time. She wouldn't believe him at first— thought he was kidding since he always ended up working through his supposed vacations. But he blocked out thirty days. He wouldn't leave Corinthia until he'd earned Dad's *and* the Williamses' forgiveness.

Hannah's sorrowful face and quivering voice flashed through his mind. How could he make amends to both his dad and Hannah? By enabling his dad to afford to move back into the main house, he would be pushing Hannah and her children out.

Chapter Four

Hannah's tears. Dad's shame.

Metal pans clanged somewhere down the hallway of the B and B as Mark flipped his Bible closed and headed out the door.

He'd gone searching for verses to strengthen him. To help him face his past. But to do so, he had to get through to his dad.

Time for a different approach. A businesslike approach. If Redd didn't want to connect on a personal level, then Mark could drop by Hometown Hardware. See how it was doing. Maybe on more neutral territory than his mother's favorite church pew or the old home place, he and his dad could find common ground.

Mark had gotten his head for business from his dad, as well as his love of tinkering and building things.

As he stood in front of the old Hometown Hardware building, a wave of nostalgia made him pause before going in. He and Matt used to love to come here. Mainly, to spend time with their dad— although he usually accused them of being underfoot and tried to shoo them to the back room. While banished to the back, Matt had preferred reading. But for Mark the tools and gadgets where Dad had set up a workshop had made the place a dream come true.

When he opened the front door, the old leather strip of sleigh bells announced his entry.

"Be right with you," Redd called across several rows of shelves.

Mark sauntered down a couple of aisles that held boxes of nails, cans of paint, packages of plumbing parts. The smell of fertilizer brought back even more memories. Nothing much had changed through the years, other than the fact that the shelves didn't seem quite as high as they once had.

"What can I do for— Mark?" His dad's welcoming smile died.

Doubt crept in. Was this another stupid mistake? "I thought I'd come by and see how the store was doing. Looks good. Well stocked. Orderly." *And I'm rambling like a fool.*

"You're still in town?"

"I'm taking some time off. Thought I'd stick around awhile."

Redd shook his head and headed for the sales counter. "Figured as much. You got fired. That's why you're here."

Mark chomped down on his automatic response that as the boss, he did any and all firing. God was still teaching him to guard his tongue. And to guard against pride. "No, sir. Just a little overdue vacation time. You taught me a strong work ethic. I don't take time off like I should."

His dad's face reddened as a scowl formed. "You saying I shoulda taken more time off?"

He and Matt had always wished their dad would take time to go fishing, go camping or even have regular meals with them. "I'm not implying anything. Just stating a fact." He put his hands in his pockets and glanced around the cash register, unnerved by his dad's scowl. "I've worked nonstop for years to get my company going, and now I've realized I could use a little time off."

A harrumph punctuated a punch to the cash register that sent the drawer clanging open. He pulled out a stack of one-dollar bills and straightened them.

Mark waited, trying to be patient, wondering if he'd been dismissed.

The front door jangled.

"Be right with you."

Yes, he'd been dismissed. He'd accomplished nothing. Yet again. "Well, Dad, I guess I'll see you around." He turned to leave. "I'm staying at the Gunters' B and B if you need anything."

Before he'd gotten far, his dad called, "So what type of company do you work at?"

A wedge formed in Mark's throat, and he had to swallow to answer. "An aeronautical engineering firm. We design unmanned aerial vehicles."

"Huh." The word didn't give a hint of the meaning behind it. "Sounds like a fancy name for remote-control toy planes."

Mark caught himself smiling. "I guess some people might think of it like that. But they're not toys. Our most recent contract uses them to safely monitor forest fires."

Redd came from behind the counter but moved toward the new customer. "I've gotta get to work. Some of us can't afford to take long vacations."

Strike three. Or had his dad maybe shown just the tiniest bit of interest?

Probably strike three. But Mark had to hold on to any chance of hope. His dad had asked him what he did at work. That was surely a move in the right direction.

His next move?

With nowhere to be, nothing to do, he'd go stir-crazy. Maybe he should put himself out into the community. Try to get reacquainted with old friends.

But what friends? Miss Ann?

Phil said she liked to spend time at the coffee shop, and he never had made it there after he ran into Becca yesterday. A visit with Ann might be nice—especially since she seemed to be the only person in town happy to see him.

Before heading that direction, he crossed the street and sat on a bench outside the courthouse. Though he was supposed to be on vacation, he had to check in. He would read his email. Then head over for that cup of decaf.

Hannah stepped into Faith's Coffee Time Café. The checkered floor gave it the feel of an old-timey ice-cream shop or diner. Tables with vases of cheery, fresh flowers and a grouping of comfy chairs made it welcoming. But, as usual, she felt out of place. She wasn't a coffee drinker. Though they served other beverages, she couldn't afford the splurge. The only time she went to the shop was to order food for bank events.

But this morning, she had ulterior motives.

A reconnaissance mission. To find out if Mark had left town as she hoped.

A very pregnant Faith stepped out from behind the counter rubbing her lower back. She was probably hitting an uncomfortable stage with the baby, but she glowed with happiness. "Hi, Hannah. Do you need to place an order for the bank?"

"No, actually, uh…I'm here on my break. I'll

try some of your hot green tea." She scanned the crowded dining room and hit pay dirt.

Ann Sealy sat at a table with her friend Jeannie, writing something in a notebook. If anyone knew the happenings in town, it would be Miss Ann. Everyone knew and loved her. And more importantly, they confided in her.

Hannah paid for the hot tea, thanked Faith, then worked her way to the little square table holding a big Bible and the kindest person Hannah knew.

"Oh, Hannah, have a seat and join us," she said in her soprano, slightly raspy, slow drawl.

"Yes, please do," Jeannie said.

Hannah nodded at the open Bible. "I don't want to interrupt."

"I've been done with my reading for a while. We've just been visiting and sharing prayer requests."

Unsure of how to jump in without sounding nosy, Hannah sat and smiled. If only Ann knew why Hannah had a stake in Mark's presence, then she—

"So what brings you by today?" Ann asked.

"Well, I wondered—"

"Ann, Jeannie!" Olivia, one of the youth's parents from the church, brushed her windblown brown hair off her face and waved madly as the front door clanged shut. "Faith, I'll have my usual," she called as she hurried over to the table.

"Oh, hello, Hannah." Olivia plopped down on a chair. "You won't believe what I just heard while I was over at Redd's."

Ann shook her head.

"I'm sure you saw who was at church yesterday in that expensive suit."

"Mark Ryker?" Ann asked.

She nodded, eyes gleaming. "So do you think the bad boy has truly made good? Because I've heard some stories about him that—" She gasped when her gaze landed on Hannah. "Oh, I'm sorry. I didn't even think about the family connection. You and your mom must've been shocked to see him."

"Shocked. Stunned. Blown away." *Angry.*

Ann gave Hannah a sympathetic look, almost as if she could see through to the true emotions darting around inside Hannah.

Olivia grimaced. "Well, I imagine the next news I have won't be pleasant, then." She leaned in as if sharing a secret. "Mark Ryker is *staying.* He's taking a long vacation."

"You don't say," Jeannie said. "I wonder what he's really doing here. Hannah, your mama must be in a tizzy."

A *long* vacation? Her heart slammed against her ribs, and the room seemed to tilt. She took a deep breath to try to steady herself. She'd made so many improvements in her children's lives in the past month. How long before he'd force them to move out?

Ann touched Hannah's cheek with a warm hand. "You okay, honey?"

"I don't know," she whispered. "I better get back to work." She couldn't tell anyone her situation. Couldn't reveal that Mark was trying to help his dad financially, trying to make sure he moved back into his house.

She couldn't tell anyone how seeing him again made her revert to old feelings of insecurity...to feeling as if she didn't matter.

She tried to shake off the crazy adolescent angst as she pushed through the coffee-shop door.

And slammed into Mark Ryker.

"Whoa!" Mark grunted as someone plowed into his chest right as he yanked open the coffee-shop door.

The *someone* looked up. Hannah.

Silky black hair brushed his hands where he held her by the shoulders, trying to steady her. "You all right?"

Bright green eyes—shocked green eyes—stared up at him. "Oh, excuse me. I didn't see you."

So beautiful. So sweet-smelling... He snatched his hands off her and shoved them into his pockets. "Totally my fault."

She didn't say anything. Just stared into his

eyes, as if trying to read him. Then the wide-eyed look gave way to skepticism…or maybe pure dislike. "I hear you're sticking around awhile."

"News travels quickly. The only person who knows outside my office is my dad."

"In this town, you're news."

He winced and rubbed the tension from the back of his neck. "I assume I'm not to take that as a compliment."

"Take it however you like." She swung her hair away from her face, going for a show of bravado.

He'd seen the move in boardroom dealings before. Never got to him at all.

Till now.

Like a punch to the gut, he realized the bravado covered pain. Pain he'd caused.

He didn't want to make her feel that way. Didn't want to upset her world any more than he already had. But he had to be truthful. "I'm taking a month of vacation time. Thought I'd try to help Dad with the house."

Her creamy ivory skin blanched. Then pink infused her cheeks. "Why?"

"As I explained before, I plan to make sure he's well cared for before I leave. Since he's not cooperating, it may take a while."

"Have you got a year of vacation time? Because that's the minimum we're staying in the house. I won't let you uproot my children." She took a deep breath as if preparing to blast him further, but instead turned and stalked toward the bank.

Mark pressed his forehead, trying to stave off a headache. Then he pushed open the café door.

The place was more crowded than he'd expected for a weekday. Most of the tables held at least one person. A group of young mothers with babies in strollers sat in some cushioned chairs in the corner.

He couldn't even remember what the building had housed when he'd been in high school. Maybe a dress shop?

Before he approached the counter, he noticed most eyes settled on him.

Oh, man. Awkward.

He smiled, then hustled to place his order.

The pregnant woman with Gabe stood behind the counter. "Welcome to my café. I'm Faith Reynolds. Relatively new to Corinthia."

He shook the hand she offered and introduced himself. "I grew up here. Went to school with Gabe."

"He told me." She glanced away, as if afraid to meet his eyes. Might reflect her husband's disdain.

His headache throbbed anew. Forget the decaf. "I'll have a large black coffee. The strongest you've got."

As she handed him the mug, she said, "I hope you and Redd can work everything out and have a nice visit." Compassionate greenish-blue eyes told him she might know a thing or two about difficult family relationships.

"Thank you. I've got a lot to make up for."

"Returning home is a start."

He accepted her small peace offering with a nod and searched for Ann.

"Oh, Mark, over here!" Miss Ann waved from a table near the window. "Come join us."

There was no "us" about it. His approach sent the other women scattering with flimsy excuses, as if he had a contagious disease. "Sorry to break up the party."

"I'm sorry they were rude." She took his hand to guide him into the seat beside her. Her soft, age-spots-speckled hand was as warm as the kindness in her blue eyes. Kindness he could use at the moment. "So, I hear tell you're going to be staying in Corinthia a while."

"Yes, ma'am. I'm taking a month off."

"Well, goodness. Have you saved up that much time?"

"Truth is, I haven't taken any vacation. So this is new for me."

"Good for you. But since you're here long-term, you can't stay at the Gunters'. It would get too expensive. Not to mention lack of privacy." She took hold of both of his hands and squeezed. "Come stay with me in my big, lonely house. Keep me company. I won't take no for an answer."

The tight grip of her hands, and the fact she gave him a "don't you dare defy me" stare, kept the refusal at bay. Surprisingly, he welcomed the idea. "I'd be honored to accept the invitation. On one condition."

"No, sir."

"Yes, ma'am. I insist you let me do any work you need done around the house. Lawn mowing, painting, repairs. I'm pretty handy, like my dad."

She gave one last squeeze, then let go. "Deal. Plan to move in tomorrow afternoon. I'll make you a nice home-cooked meal and one of my caramel cakes."

His mouth practically watered at the thought. He winked at her. "I look forward to it."

Maybe things were looking up after all.

One look at the woman across the street, and Mark's good mood evaporated like raindrops on a sizzling summer sidewalk.

Donna Williams. Sitting on the same bench Mark had occupied earlier to check his email. Staring a hole through him while Hannah's children played in the center of the town square, out in front of the courthouse.

Time to face the music.

He crossed the street as she gathered Hannah's

children under her wing, as if he was some villain who might make off with them.

"Hi, Mr. Mark," Becca called as she ran up to him, beaming. "We're going to the library."

"Sounds fun." He greeted the other children, then nodded to Donna. "Mrs. Williams."

The two youngest looked so much alike. He realized they were twins. An ache tugged at his chest as the boy pulled on one pant leg.

The girl tugged on the other. "We're going to check out books."

"I'm getting the biggest book ever." The boy let go of Mark's leg, stretched to his tiptoes and held his arms wide. "This big."

The older boy, with his unruly sandy-brown hair, looked from Mark to his grandmother and back. As if he sensed the tension.

Donna pulled the little ones away from Mark. "Children, why don't you all hold hands and walk on over to the library. Do what Becca tells you to do. I'll be there in a minute. After I talk to Mr. Ryker."

He realized his teeth were clenched and forcefully relaxed as the kids grabbed hands and scampered off, Becca acting like a proud mother hen.

Donna crossed her arms, her disapproving glare like a blast of frigid air across the sidewalk. "Why aren't you gone yet?"

Not only had he hurt Sydney years ago, but now

his presence must dredge up old pain. "I've decided to stay, maybe do some work on the house."

"So your father can move back in?"

"I admit, I don't like the idea of my father living in a garage apartment with those steep steps and his bad hip. Especially when he's nearing retirement."

Donna threw her arms out to her sides. "I warned Hannah. Told her to stay away from that place. From associating with *you Rykers*." She took a step closer and pointed a finger in his face. "Don't you dare hurt my other daughter, too. You just need to go on back to the city. Your daddy can take care of himself."

Tell her, Mark. She might listen. "Actually, Mrs. Williams, I've come to try to make amends with my father. And hope you, too, will forgive me for getting Sydney involved with a bad crowd. With alcohol."

She stepped back, and the firm composure crumbled. "I don't know how you have the nerve to even ask. You have no idea what your actions did to my family."

"Hannah told me. Please believe me when I say I had no idea the pain I'd caused." He shoved his hands into his pockets and looked skyward for some divine help. "God has changed my life. I'm so very sorry for hurting your family."

"You think you can just blow into town and say

you're sorry? And that'll fix everything? Well, I've got news for you. *Nothing* will ever fix the mess you made." She took two steps but then stopped. "Stay away from my family."

As she stormed down the street, Mark trudged to his car.

Maybe some sins were too hard for people to forgive. He was probably just wasting his time by trying.

But God had brought him this far. He would keep praying God would soften their hearts.

Meanwhile, he would get to work on his dad's house.

Chapter Five

Hannah appreciated the few moments of peace her tree-lined driveway afforded. Especially when she was limp as a dishrag after the day she'd had at the bank. Especially after the earful her mother had just given, informing her she'd warned Mark away from their family.

She sighed as they chugged along, wondering how slowly she could drive, how long she could stretch out the quiet before the kids would notice.

The thought brought a smile. She looked forward to a nice evening at home with her children. She'd cook something healthy—maybe make the chicken-casserole recipe from the church ladies' cookbook. Then she'd make sure she had fifteen minutes alone with each child to hear about their day. To make each one feel special.

"Look, a car," Tony called as they drove into the clearing.

"And there's Mr. Mark," Becca said, opening the door a nanosecond after they'd come to a complete stop.

"Becca, hold up." *What in the world?*

Mark Ryker. In her side yard, sanding something that lay across a sawhorse, almost punishing the wood.

Or himself.

His sweat-soaked T-shirt strained across broad, muscular shoulders. His old, faded jeans were streaked with dirt. Her traitorous heart thrilled at the sight.

She must be crazy to find this man attractive.

The kids spilled out of the car, calling his name. She followed, not nearly as excited to have him there.

While the kids surrounded him, chattering a mile a minute, he looked right at her. Anger or hurt—or both—filled his eyes when he first spotted her. Then he quickly covered it. He looked away and spoke to the kids. But she'd seen the raw emotion.

The stubble of his beard gave him a dangerous look, and she could feel his tension. He might be a well-off, successful business owner, but she would not want to run into him in a back alley. Rumor had it that he'd lived on the streets for a while. She now had no trouble believing it.

She drew closer, determined to hurry the children inside. And to hurry him away.

Becca tugged on Mark's shirt and pointed to her siblings. "Mr. Mark, you don't know all their names. This is my brother Tony. He's seven."

"Nice to meet you, Tony."

"Hi." Tony didn't look up. Instead, he rubbed his hand over the wood, checking out Mark's work.

"And this is my brother Eric and sister, Emily." Becca puffed up proudly. "They're both six."

He squatted down in front of the two of them and looked back and forth. "Let me guess. Twins?"

Emily squealed, "You're right." Then she threw her arms around his neck.

Not to be outdone, Eric launched himself into the other outstretched arm. "How could you tell?"

Hannah would have been bowled over if they'd thrown themselves on her. But strong as a tree, Mark stood firm. "Could be the fact that you look a whole lot alike. Or maybe that you're both six years old."

Emily giggled. "You're smart, Mr. Mark."

Hannah's chest constricted. The kids were starved for a man's attention. Needed their dad. But why did they have to be so taken with Mark?

"Time to go wash your hands, you four. I'll even let you help me with dinner." She handed Becca the key.

Peals of joy affirmed her offer. Cooking proved enticing enough to pull them away from the mysterious Mr. Mark and into the house.

"I'll be finished here soon. Will get out of your way," he said as he wiped the shoulder of his shirt across his face.

"Sanding the shutters?"

"Yes, and painting them. Most needed securing anyway."

Though the prospect of having the place look half-decent tempted her, she wasn't going to encourage the man to hang around. Not when having him nearby made her pulse scatter. Not when looking into those beautiful golden eyes did strange things to her insides. And certainly not when her children were as drawn to him as she was. "Well, I need to go make dinner." Fighting the urge to turn and run, she nodded goodbye.

He nodded back and returned to his work, apparently taking her mother's warning to heart. She had little sympathy for most of her mom's gripes, but in Mark's case, Donna was justified.

As soon as Hannah had changed into shorts and a T-shirt, she rounded up the kids and explained the recipe. They would boil the chicken, then shred it for the casserole. She pulled out a large pot and went to the refrigerator. *Butter, sour cream...*

She rooted all the way to the back of the shelves.

"You're kidding me. I thought I laid out chicken to thaw." She wanted to slap her forehead as she remembered she hadn't found any chicken in the freezer yesterday. And had never gone to the store.

She groaned.

"I didn't really want chicken anyway," Becca said, probably trying to make Hannah feel better. Then again, chicken never thrilled Becca.

"What are we going to do?" Tony asked.

Hannah blinked back tears. She rarely had time to prepare wholesome home-cooked meals like good parents should. Tonight she'd counted on it. But had failed again.

"Can we have pasghetti again?" Emily asked.

Hannah sighed and shook her head. "No, sweetie. I imagine the others are sick of spaghetti."

Becca darted out of the kitchen. "Be right back."

As Hannah put all the other ingredients away, heavy footsteps—and the click of dog nails—sounded down the hardwood floors of the hallway, coming toward the kitchen.

Hannah sucked in a breath. When Becca came in holding Mark's hand, followed by Blue, she let it out in a rush.

"Rebecca Lyn, did you disturb Mr. Mark while he's working?"

"I hear you need to make a run to the grocery store. I'll be glad to go get that chicken."

A crooked smile conveyed he knew she was not happy with her daughter at the moment.

"Oh, good. I don't want watery pa...spaghetti again," Eric said.

Hannah tried not to huff or roll her eyes. Or cry from embarrassment. "No, but thank you for your offer. We'll make do." With peanut butter and jelly. Again. Once more, tears threatened. She shooed the dog away and then yanked the loaf of bread out of the cabinet—a reason to turn away from Mark. She was a horrible mother.

"I promise, it's no bother," he said. "I'm cleaning up now."

Becca jumped up and down in excitement. "Let him, Mom. Then he can come back and eat with us."

The blood drained from Hannah's face clear to her toes, leaving her dizzy.

"Oh, no, I can't impose. I've got to go back to the inn and pack. Ann Sealy has invited me to stay there while I'm in town."

"Please, Mr. Mark? I really want chicken tonight." Becca flashed a smile in Hannah's direction, trying to butter her up after having stretched the truth.

"I can make a quick trip for that chicken. It's up to your mom."

"No." She would not be beholden to the man.

Realizing the refusal had been snippy, she added, "Thank you, though. We'll make sandwiches."

"Gross," Eric and Emily said at the same time, as if on cue.

"I really wanted chicken." Tony sighed as he left the kitchen with the twins following behind.

Becca pushed up her glasses and stared at the two of them.

"Well, I'll get going, then." He waved and was gone.

"Becca, you are not to ask for favors or invite people over without checking with me first."

"But aren't we supposed to love our neighbors?" She looked up, so serious and tenderhearted.

Hannah sometimes wished she could simply sneak away for a nice hot bubble bath with a book to read. This was one of those moments—which made her more ashamed of herself. "Yes, we are. But you always have to ask me privately first. Plus, this is supposed to be family night. He's not part of our family."

Becca crossed her arms and put on her stubborn face. "I bet Pastor Phil would say we should invite him." Then she stomped out of the kitchen, leaving Hannah to prepare their makeshift dinner alone.

She grabbed the peanut-butter jar. Pulled the grape-jelly squeeze bottle out of the refrigerator. Then reached for the loaf of bread.

But it wasn't there.

Hadn't she already pulled it out? She opened the cabinet. Sure enough, no bread.

She marched to the bottom of the stairs and hollered up toward the bedrooms. "Who has the loaf of bread?"

They all denied knowing anything.

Determined to feed her children, she reached for a box of Cheerios. Not only was she failing to make that home-cooked meal, but she must also be losing her mind.

Mark finished putting away the tools he'd borrowed from the garage and was about to leave when he spotted Blue with his muzzle inside a plastic bag. On closer inspection, he realized it was a bread bag. Or had been. Now it was a bag of bread crumbs covered in dog slobber.

He closed his eyes and laughed. *Uh-oh.* Would Hannah blame him for letting the dog inside?

The thought of the family trying to make sandwiches, and then finding they had no bread, made the decision for him.

He'd make the trip to the grocery store for Hannah.

He hurried to town, grabbed the family-size pack of chicken and a loaf of bread. Then he realized how late it would be by the time she cooked it. So he also picked up already-cooked rotisserie chickens and several side dishes. On the way to the checkout line, he nabbed a huge box of Twinkies for the kids' dessert.

"Having a craving?" asked a woman he'd seen at church, though he couldn't remember her name.

"A craving?" He glanced down at the box. "Oh." With a laugh, he said, "No, these are for the Hughes kids."

"Oh, I see." By the time she finished her sentence, her eyebrows were up in the vicinity of her hairline.

Uh-oh. "Hannah had an incident with her dinner preparations. And I happened to be at the house working. And...well..."

The woman's expression said she wasn't buying his excuses. So he smiled and set his items on the checkout counter.

When he got back to the house, Blue was gone, but the bread bag was still lying in the yard. Apparently, Hannah hadn't discovered the dog's mischief.

He smiled as he rang the front doorbell.

When Hannah opened the door and spied the shopping bags, her mouth fell open. "You went anyway?"

Becca peeked around her mom, then shot her a smug, satisfied look. "See, Mom. Neighbors do help each other." All of a sudden, she gasped and pointed out toward the yard. "There's the bread!"

Hannah's eyes narrowed as she zeroed in on the empty plastic. "That dog…" She stomped down the front steps and yanked up the trash. Apparently, she had made contact with the slobber, because she wrinkled her nose and tried to grasp it by the edge.

When she barreled back up the steps, he held out the grocery bags. "I saw what was left of your bread out front. Knew you couldn't make sandwiches without it. You might need to teach your dog some manners."

"I'll have you know that's your dad's dog," she snipped. Color crept up her cheeks and looked good on her.

He bit back a smile. "Guess he needs to work on it, then." She still hadn't taken the bags from him. "Can I carry this in for you?"

He wouldn't be surprised if steam blew out her ears any second. But she nodded anyway. "Thank you."

Those words had cost her. As a person who hated to ever ask for help, he understood.

When he entered the kitchen, he found she had pulled out bowls and a box of cereal. Again, he fought a grin.

He had to admire her. Working full-time and caring for four kids alone must be overwhelming. If he had to do it alone, they'd probably eat fast food at every meal.

"You came just in time," Becca said. "We're out of milk, so we couldn't have cereal, either."

"Becca," Hannah scolded. She was probably embarrassed.

"Hey, I love to cook but never have ingredients on hand when I need them. I understand."

Hannah stared into his eyes for a moment, as if deciding whether he was telling the truth or trying to make her feel better. Then she quickly looked away. "Thank you."

"What'd ya bring, Mr. Mark?"

"Well, the chicken your mom needed. Also some chicken that's already cooked." He pulled out the Twinkies and presented the box to Becca. "And dessert."

"Woo hoo!" She grabbed the box and took off to show her siblings. "Thank you," she called as she hurried away.

Hannah looked as if she were choking on a big chicken bone.

Not wanting to irritate her further, he said, "Gotta run. I hope this makes up for what that silly dog did."

"Stay." The command came out harshly. For some reason, it struck him as funny.

"Is that an invitation? Or a dog command?"

Red flamed across her cheeks, but then she jumped into motion, unpacking the grocery bags.

"You were kind enough to bring dinner. Stay and eat with us."

Ah, yes. Good manners, dictated by the duty to reciprocate. A Southern law. For some reason, he wanted to accept the offer, just to test it, to see how she would respond.

And maybe because I'd love to share a meal with Hannah and her children?

A stampede of footsteps pounded down the stairs and into the kitchen, distracting him from unwanted thoughts.

"Can you stay and eat with us, Mr. Mark?" Emily asked.

"Yeah, Mr. Mark. We'll even let you have a Twinkies," Eric added.

"Shh." Becca held her finger over her mouth. "You're supposed to ask Mom first."

As much as he'd like to test the offer of hospitality, he had to remember this wasn't a friendly game of irritate-your-neighbor. This woman and her family had taken over Redd's house, leaving him to traipse up and down those garage steps. Mark meant to follow through with his plans. But that left a new dilemma of how to help Hannah find another place to live at the end of the contract. Or better yet, as soon as possible.

"I appreciate the kind offer." He looked into Hannah's green eyes and thought maybe he saw a spark of humor. "But I can't."

She did smile then, a smile of relief, and maybe a touch of victory.

Unable to resist a bit of fun at her expense, he knelt down in front of the twins. "I tell you what. I'll take you up on that offer another time, though. I'd love to taste that chicken recipe when your mom makes it." He pulled out a business card and gave it to Becca. "Give this to your mom and have her call me next time you're having chicken. Okay?"

"Sure, Mr. Mark!"

He winked at Hannah—his own show of victory. But as he walked out, he knew he'd made a tactical error. Getting involved with this family. Even if he did find a suitable place for them to live, how would he be able to follow through on asking them to leave?

Hannah found her mom pacing the front sidewalk of her house the next day when she went to pick up her kids.

Had something happened to one of them? She flew out of the minivan. "Mom, what's wrong?"

She whirled around and stopped. "That man has been at your house. He bought you groceries." She got in Hannah's face. "Please tell me nothing's going on between you."

"That's ridiculous." Yes, ridiculous. Admiring his beautiful eyes and muscled arms didn't constitute something going on between them. "He happened to see that the dog had eaten part of our dinner, so he brought us some groceries. Against my wishes, I might add."

Donna's shoulders relaxed, and her head fell back. "Thank You, God. I was so worried he would get to you, too, with his good looks and charm."

"You worry too much." She hollered for the kids, and they piled into the van. "Thanks for babysitting. Will you come to our house tomorrow?"

Donna rolled her eyes. "You ask that every day. What do you think my answer is?"

"I can always hope you'll change your mind."

As Hannah and the kids pulled out of the parking spot, Becca's stomach growled loud enough for all to hear. She laughed. "Can we have chicken tonight?"

"Becca Hughes, you never ask for chicken. How about pork chops? I can stop at the store and get some."

"Won't the chicken get old and gross if we don't eat it soon?"

Hannah turned and raised her brows at her oldest daughter. "I can freeze it."

"Why don't you like Mr. Mark?"

"Yeah, Mom. You're not very nice to him," Tony added.

They were way too young to hear the truth about Mark Ryker. "I'll try to be nicer."

There. Topic closed.

Becca giggled. "Good. Then he can eat chicken with us tonight."

Was she really only nine years old? How could a child look so innocent while manipulating her own mother?

Hannah made a U-turn and headed back toward town. "I guess we can't serve him Twinkies." With all the groceries he'd bought, she could afford to splurge. She drove to Faith's Coffee Time Café to pick up dessert.

They walked inside, and while the kids oohed and aahed over the dessert choices in the pastry display case, Hannah walked over to a table to speak to Jeannie. Frederica Smith sat with her.

Frederica's deceased mother, Maude, had been a longtime active church member. But her daughter had fallen away. Jeannie had been trying to mentor her.

"Hey, there, Hannah. Picking up some pastries?" Jeannie asked.

"Yes. Wanted a decent dessert tonight."

"For company?" Frederica tried to look nonchalant, but Hannah could tell she was fishing.

"The kids love Faith's brownies." There, that was evasive enough. And truthful.

Jeannie took Hannah's hand and pulled her into

a chair. "I don't mean to butt in. But I have to tell you this. For your own good."

Frederica nodded her agreement as she gave Hannah a sympathetic look.

Had word already gotten out about Mark being at her house? The more talk buzzed about, the more agitated Donna would get. The drama was enough to tie Hannah's stomach in knots. "So what is it?"

"We heard Mark Ryker has moved in with Ann," Jeannie said. "Of course, she says she invited him, but we're afraid he might take advantage of her hospitality."

Frederica's frown deepened. "And we heard he's trying to hang around you—of all people. As if he didn't do enough damage to your family already."

"Ladies, I assure you, he's not trying to hang around me. He just happened to be working on a project at Redd's house when I had a dinner disaster."

"Well, he's mooching off Ann," Jeannie added.

Hannah knew good and well he had plenty of funds and didn't need to mooch. These women were being gossipy. "Mark owns a successful business, so I'm sure he doesn't need handouts." Now, why was she defending the man? They would think she had a thing for him.

Jeannie patted her hand. "Just be careful. He's a charmer. Always has been, always will be."

"I promise I'll be careful. Better run before the kids order everything in the display case."

Were Jeannie and Frederica being unforgiving, untrusting? Or were they rightly cautious?

As she and the kids left with their bag of goodies, Hannah wondered if God was speaking to her through the ladies...and even her mom. Was she playing with fire by trying to model a good example to her children in letting them invite Mark to dinner?

With the hot evening sun beating down on his back, Mark hammered one last nail into the newly restored shutter, hanging it in place on the upper level. He'd moved his sawhorse to the far side of the house, hoping his dad wouldn't see him. Hoping he wouldn't notice the refurbished shutters until Mark had had a chance to establish their relationship on better terms. With the way things stood now, Redd might try to kick him off the property.

He climbed down the ladder to see how the shutter looked.

"What do you think you're doing?"

Jolted by the sudden intrusion, Mark yanked his head around and found his dad standing with arms crossed.

"I'm making some repairs to the house since I've got time on my hands."

"Your help isn't welcome."

If Redd didn't want Mark slapping up a little paint, what would he do when he discovered the deposit in his bank account? "Well, I kind of figured that. That's why I didn't ask first."

Redd looked away and over Mark's shoulder. "I know the place needs work. You can leave with the assurance I'll do it when I have the time."

"Like when you retire?"

He nodded. "Yeah. Sure."

Mark crossed his arms and then realized he was a mirror image of his dad. He uncrossed them and jammed his hands into his jeans pockets, trying to look as if this conversation didn't have him as nervous as the day he signed the first government contract for his planes. "Dad, this is your home. You should be heading into retirement in comfort. Not in some garage apartment with steep steps to climb."

"I'm fine in the garage. Hardly ever home anyway. And I like having Hannah and the kids around."

"They've put you out of the house your grandfather built."

"No, they haven't. They answered my ad. It could be anyone renting right now. I just lucked out. It's nice having the sound of kids' laughter again."

The jab hit right where his dad had aimed it.

Or at least where Mark thought he'd aimed. No matter, the guilt over Matt's death knocked him breathless. And speechless.

He moved his ladder to the other side of the porch. He could practically hear Matt's voice, laughing, yelling across the yard, asking him to come throw the baseball with him.

But that had been a lifetime ago. After Matt's death, there had only been silence. Silence as his mom took to her bed in grief. Silence as his dad hid out at the hardware store. Silence as Mark tried to make amends but couldn't. Once he accepted that fact, he'd stayed out of everyone's way.

Laughter sounded again, and when his dad looked toward the driveway, Mark realized it wasn't just an echo from the past. Hannah's kids had come home.

The twins ran to hug Redd. Becca and Tony hurried over to Mark and seemed truly happy to see him. He swallowed a sudden lump from his throat as he ruffled Tony's hair and tweaked Becca's pigtail.

Becca looked up and grinned. "You have to eat with us tonight. We're having chicken that you bought, and we got brownies and cookies and Mom said it's okay and that she'll try to be nice." She sucked in an audible breath. "So will you stay? Huh?"

She'll try to be nice! Before he could fully register the request, Becca turned to his dad. "And you, too, Mr. Redd. Please stay and eat with us."

Redd looked at Mark as he answered. "You kids are really nice to invite me, but I can't come over tonight. Maybe another time." The expression on his face told Mark he better refuse, too.

The fact that his own father might be trying to protect Hannah's family from him socked him in the gut.

He knelt down in front of Becca and Tony. "I better not stay, either. Miss Ann will be expecting me."

Hannah came around the front of the van just then, jacket thrown across her arm, blouse sleeves rolled up. Her cheeks were flushed. She looked tired. Stressed.

Becca tugged on his T-shirt. "But you said you'd eat with us when we had the chicken. And I don't even like chicken. But I asked Mom to make it so we can have dinner with you." Her sad brown eyes nearly undid him.

Hannah took Becca's hand. "It's okay, sweetie. I imagine Miss Ann has already started dinner." She reached for Tony. "Come on, kids, let the men get back to work."

Becca's head turned as her mom pulled her toward the house, and she gave Mark a pitiful look.

How could he disappoint them? They'd even

gotten dessert just for him. "I tell you what. Let me call Miss Ann to check."

As he pulled out his cell phone, Hannah ushered the cheering kids inside. The wariness on her face as she followed them through the back door told him Hannah didn't trust him.

Redd shook his head in disgust. "I don't know if you're playing games or if you just aren't using your head. Either way, you better not hurt those kids. Or Hannah. You'll have to answer to me if you do." After a quick glance at the door, he turned and started toward the garage. "Oh, and leave the home repairs to me. I'm perfectly capable of taking care of my own property."

Mark couldn't win.

But no matter what Redd and Hannah thought, he would not disappoint a sweet nine-year-old girl who was willing to eat chicken for him.

Broad shoulders dominated the kitchen. Hannah couldn't think straight. She'd reached for the salt instead of the butter and barely caught herself before sprinkling the rolls. How could one strong pair of shoulders knock her so off balance?

She wanted nothing more than to tolerate a meal with Mark—and try to be nice in front of the kids. But having him crowd her kitchen was making her a nervous wreck.

"I just need a few more minutes before the meal

is ready," she said as she brushed past him to pull the casserole out of the oven. When he reached to help her, she stopped him with a hot-mitt-gloved hand. "I've got it. Why don't you go sit in the family room for a few minutes? Visit with the kids. I'll call you when dinner is ready."

He chuckled. "Ah, okay. I'm in the way. Sorry."

With an embarrassed smile, she pointed him in the right direction. As soon as he walked out, she took a deep breath, trying to ease some of the tension from the room. The man made her skittish. Of course, he always had, even when he was a teenager. Maybe his good looks were to blame. Or the quiet confidence. Or those intense eyes and the way he watched her. Maybe it was the intensity with which he did everything.

Or maybe she just needed to get a grip.

Once she had the food on the table, she went to the family room to gather everyone. All was quiet, so she peeked in.

Mark sat in the chair with the twins squeezed in, Eric on one side, Emily on the other. Becca lounged at his feet. Though Tony sat across the room playing a handheld video game, she saw him glance in Mark's direction several times.

They were all blissfully unaware of Mark's tension as he read them a story. Hannah could tell by the set of his shoulders how he seemed to shrink in on himself, trying to stay in his part of the seat.

She smiled at his unease as Emily and Eric, totally relaxed, leaned on him. Before long, though, Mark warmed to the story, raising his voice to talk like a girl dragon, then lowering it to talk like the wise grandfather dragon. By the time he finished, he'd loosened up. Comfortable with two little ones hanging on him and Becca staring up with adoring eyes.

The air seemed to freeze in her lungs, making it difficult to breathe.

Seeing her children so happy with Mark, seeing how gentle he was with them and seeing how her life could be if she had a man in it set off an ache in her belly that darted to her heart.

She stepped fully into the room. "Time to eat." A forced smile accompanied the announcement. "Kids, go wash up."

Mark seemed…almost disappointed when they popped up off his lap. But as soon as the children washed their hands, they hurried to the kitchen.

"I call sitting by Mr. Mark!" Becca pulled out the chair at the end of the table and tried to steer him into it.

"I'd be honored," he said as he pulled out Becca's chair for her. "But ladies first."

She giggled as she sat and allowed him to push the chair in. He did the same for Emily.

Then he pulled out the only chair left and

waited, brows raised as he stared at Hannah. His crooked smile made her heart thud.

She tried not to notice how good he smelled as she sat. Faintly like fresh, tangy cologne. Faintly like sunshine.

When he finally took his seat, he ended up directly across from Hannah, the two of them at opposite ends of the rectangular table.

"Let's say a blessing. It's Tony's turn." She waited until the kids folded their hands and bowed their heads. Tony said a quick prayer he'd learned years back during preschool.

When he'd finished, Mark said, "Nice job."

Her oldest son beamed as they passed the food. Hannah noticed Becca wrinkling her nose when the chicken casserole reached her. "Becca, honey, go look in the microwave."

When she discovered the hotdog Hannah had prepared for her, she giggled and clapped her hands. "Thank you, Mom."

"Oh, I see. So you invited me over for chicken, but you're having a hotdog." Mark grinned at her as he scooped out chicken for himself. "What if I prefer hotdogs?"

Becca's eyes widened. Then she held out the hotdog, offering it to him.

A hearty laugh burst out of him. "I'm just teasing. I wouldn't dream of taking your hotdog. This chicken looks delicious. My mom used to make something similar."

"Probably so," Hannah said. "It's a recipe out of the old church cookbook."

"Maybe my mom's recipe." He didn't look up after he said it. Instead, he forked food into his mouth.

But she could tell speaking about his mother was painful.

Becca chomped into the hotdog; then she grinned up at Mark. "Mmm."

The rest of the meal went like normal in the Hughes household. Eric and Emily got in a scuffle over the rolls. Tony picked anything that had color and was the least bit healthy out of his food—and offered it to Mark, who didn't bat an eye but gracefully declined. Yet it was totally *not* normal. Having Mark at the table changed everything. Because it felt almost…natural.

Once they'd finished, as Hannah cleared the dishes, she fought a huge sigh that wanted to escape. She had let her guard down. Dangerous business. She wanted to be wary, yet at the moment, she felt drawn to Mark, to his kindness, to his obvious need for companionship—a need she was starting to feel again herself as she slowly healed.

She could tell he'd enjoyed the time at her table. Had enjoyed time with her children.

That sigh slipped out.

"Here. Let me help clean up." He swiped the dishrag from her and took over washing the baking dish.

Pausing, she observed his profile, the strong, square jaw, tanned face, areas of sun-lightened hair from time spent outdoors. Warmth crept through her, making her want to smile, to stand near him and chat about the day while they worked side by side.

She shook the thought out of her head and busied herself putting away leftovers.

How had eating a meal with Mark Ryker changed her perspective so much? As if dipping into the same casserole dish or sharing a plate of brownies made it impossible to see him as a villain. She suddenly saw him as...well, as a real person.

How could she possibly hate Mark now that he'd bragged on her chicken casserole and had joked with Becca over the hotdog?

How could she look at him as the bad guy now that he'd sat in a recliner with Emily and Eric crawling all over him?

How could she resist that certain *something* that drew her to him now that he'd responded, without batting an eye, as Tony offered him each bit of celery he plucked from his casserole—with his fingers?

The kids played in the next room, leaving Mark and her alone in the kitchen. The quiet drove her crazy, allowing her wild thoughts free rein.

Enough. "My turn." She tried to take back the dishcloth, but the attempt left her pressed up against Mark's side, their hands tangling in the soapy water.

He held firmly. "I've got it. You must be worn-out."

She yanked away from him and dried her hands. "I'm fine. Not much left to do."

He grabbed the scrubber sponge and attacked the last of the baked-on chicken. "I don't see how you do it all."

When he finally handed her the clean casserole dish, she began to dry. "It was difficult in the beginning, but I'm getting used to it. I try to stick to a routine, but…well, life gets in the way."

"Do you ever get lonely?"

She lifted smaller baking dishes out of the cabinet and nested them in the newly washed one. "Most of the time I'm too busy to think about it. But sometimes…like my birthday…or Valentine's Day…" She put the stack back in the cabinet. Snapped the door shut. Glanced into his eyes. "I'll admit this past Valentine's I was whiney and felt sorry for myself."

He grabbed the dirty baking sheet she'd used

to warm the rolls and plunged it in the water, encouraging her with a smile to tell more.

She laughed as she shook her head. "All that day I wished for a knight in shining armor to whisk me away. To shower me with flowers and jewels."

He laughed, too. Still, she felt silly for admitting it. "Dumb, I know. But, hey, a girl can dream, can't she?"

His laughter died, but a smile remained. "Not dumb at all. I have a few crazy dreams myself." He stared into her eyes for a moment before glancing away.

"Such as…?"

"Making my dad proud." He said it quickly and passionately. Then he turned away and busied himself washing the baking sheet, color streaking across his cheeks.

She focused her attention on putting the last plate into the dishwasher to give him a moment. "Yes, dreams are good. Most of the time, though, I live in my reality—single mom of four amazing kids."

"I think *you're* pretty amazing." He gave her a crooked grin. "For someone who used to be a pesky kid."

She swiped the damp dishcloth from his hand and smacked him on the arm with it. "I was never pesky. Skulking and nosy, yes. But never pesky," she said with a laugh.

The laugh faded. Awkwardness took over as they both remembered why they had been in each other's company back then. Sydney.

She washed the last serving bowl and pulled the plug from the bottom of the sink. Water rushed down the drain. If only she could rid her mind of the past so easily.

"Are you a bookworm like you were in middle school?" he asked.

"I wish I had time to read. But as you can see, Becca is following in my footsteps."

"She's a cute kid. They all are."

Hannah dried her hands and hung up the dish towel. "Thanks. They're wonderful. They've kept me going the last two years since my husband died."

He leaned against the counter and crossed his ankles, hands in his pockets, in that same relaxed, country-club pose she'd loathed the other day. Only this time, it looked good on him.

"I'm really sorry about your husband. How did he die?"

"Cancer."

Shaking his head, he looked at the floor, then up at her. "How are your children doing?"

"As well as can be expected. The twins were very young. And though Becca is older, she's handled it pretty well. But I worry about Tony. He's the most sensitive of the four and really misses having a man around." She darted a glance at him, wishing she hadn't said the last comment. Hoping he didn't think she was asking for anything from him. "Having your dad around seems to have helped. Tony is slowly warming up to him."

"I'm glad." Mark pushed away from the counter. "I should go. Thanks for a delicious dinner."

Saying she'd enjoyed herself despite the fact she shouldn't have didn't seem prudent. "Thanks for supplying the chicken. I'm just relieved Blue didn't take off with anything."

He laughed, then settled into a friendly smile, his golden eyes warm and sparkling. For a moment, she thought he was going to say something else, but then he headed out of the kitchen.

She leaned against the door frame and listened as he said goodbye to the children. She could tell he made a point to find each one, going as far as to holler upstairs to locate Tony. Tony's footsteps sounded along the hallway overhead, then he stopped at the top of the stairs to say goodbye.

Then the front door opened and closed.

No matter what Mark had done in the past, he was not a bad man. Yet she couldn't wrap her head around it.

One thing she could grasp, though, was that she

better guard her heart. She had to think of the re-
percussions if she fell for him like Sydney had.

"Oh, Hannah, honey, I'm sorry to hear that. Can
I help?" Ann said into the phone as Mark was
heading out the front door.

The name *Hannah* stopped him. That and the
fact that it must be bad news, from the tone of
Ann's voice.

He'd risen early, planning to work at the house
and be gone before his dad finished at the store.
But first he had to find out what was going on.

"I'll be glad to. Will be there as soon as I can
get out of these slippers and put on my shoes."

By the time she hung up, Mark stood beside her.
"Is everything okay with Hannah and the kids?"

"Yes. Donna has a bad migraine and can't
babysit. Hannah is already late for work. I'm
going over as soon as I can get ready."

He wasn't certain Ann had the energy to watch
four kids all day long. "You were planning to
attend your Bible study today. I was going over
to work on the house anyway. Why don't I watch
them?"

Her eyes brightened, but then an extra crease
formed in her forehead. "I should probably call
her back and check."

"If she prefers having you, I'll let you know."

Once Ann had agreed and extracted a promise

from him that he wouldn't take his eyes off the kids for a second, he hurried to his dad's house.

Hannah raced out the door, but then stopped in her tracks when she spotted him. "Oh, I thought you were Ann."

"I am. Or, rather, I'm here in her place. I was walking out the door to come work on the house when you called, so I offered to watch the gang."

He'd never seen a person so still. She didn't seem to breathe as she considered his declaration. "Have you ever babysat before?"

"Well…no. But I'm sure I'm capable. I'll let them help me on the house."

"Oh, they can't help you work. Someone will get hurt."

"I was thinking more along the lines of painting the fence. I loved to paint when I was a boy."

Obviously torn, she glanced at her watch and then squinted up at him with a pained expression on her face.

"I'll call if I need you."

"Do you promise to call Ann if you can't handle them?"

"Of course. We'll be fine."

She opened her van door and started to climb in. Then she popped back out. "No macho-man stunts—like getting on the roof or up a ladder. No power tools. Or—"

He laughed as he guided her back into the vehicle. "No testosterone-driven moves, I promise. Only kid-friendly activities."

She sat looking into his eyes, as if deciding whether she could trust him.

After last night, he had hope. Hope they'd become friends. Or that they had at least built a little trust.

He'd probably enjoyed himself too much. And looked forward too much to the opportunity to babysit. But beyond his own feelings, he was glad he was available to help when she needed it.

The worry cleared from her eyes. "Okay."

After entering their cell-phone numbers into each other's phones, she nodded. "Thank you."

Her tires crunched down the driveway as he approached the house. The door flew open, and the kids ran out.

They slammed on their brakes when they saw him.

"Are you watching us today?" Becca asked.

Four expectant faces gave him pause. A wave of apprehension tightened his neck muscles. But what trouble could a handful of kids be? "I am. And I have a job for you."

Within a half hour, he had them happily painting the fence that ran along the right side of the house. Other than the fact that Becca preferred painting designs and flourishes, and the twins enjoyed painting each other, all went well.

Conscientious Tony made sure every inch was covered, going behind his siblings to perfect their work.

About eleven o'clock, they said they were hungry, so they went inside and made peanut-butter-and-jelly sandwiches. Mark had a feeling Hannah would show up sooner or later to check on them, so he suggested they make her a lunch, as well.

They rushed through their meal, eager to paint some more. The four were back at it and happy as larks when Redd drove up at noon.

"Hi, Mr. Redd," Becca called.

He lumbered over to inspect. "Helping Mark paint, huh? He used to do that when he was your age."

"Yep," Tony said. "Look how good we're doing."

"I'm impressed. You're all doing a fine job."

Mark was waiting for his dad to tell him to get lost, to find something else to do with his time. Of course, he wouldn't do that in front of the Hughes kids. "Donna is sick today," he explained. "Ann was going to come, but I offered."

"Since you were going to be working on the house anyway?"

Mark sensed the unvoiced finish to that sentence—*even though I told you not to.*

"Dad, I really do want to help. I hope you'll let me."

"Mr. Mark, look! I finished this whole section

by myself." Tony stood and pointed, eyes bright green like his mother's, glowing with pride. "See? I didn't miss a spot. And no drips."

Mark knelt down in front of the boy and inspected. Then he whistled. "Sure looks good." He gave him a high five. "Nice job."

"Thanks." Beaming, Tony moved on to the next section.

"You got anything to feed them for lunch?" Redd asked, his voice gruff and irritated.

"Already ate sandwiches."

He harrumphed. But then he stared at Tony, watching him dip the brush and apply the paint in long, even strokes. "That's more words than I've heard the boy say in quite a while. Don't see many of those smiles, either." He glanced at Mark. Then his gaze darted off toward the house. "Guess I won't stop you from doing some work around the place if you're determined."

Mark didn't know what to say. Before he could say anything, his dad stomped off toward the garage and went inside. A few minutes later he came out with a stack of file folders and drove off.

Maybe they could gradually rebuild trust.

He heard his dad honk at the green minivan pulling up the driveway. Hannah, coming to check on them. He didn't fault her, though. Wouldn't he do the same if he were her? "Kids, wave to your mom."

They squealed with joy as they flagged her down to see their work.

She didn't get out, just cruised up next to them. "Wow. You've been busy."

They each showed her the sections they'd worked on, but Mark noticed how she studied Tony the longest.

Mark walked over to the van. "See, they're all in one piece. No blood. No broken bones."

She laughed even as she watched Tony. "Okay. You proved me wrong. I'll go back to work and quit worrying."

"Wait! We've got you something." Becca zipped inside the front door, then came running back with the brown lunch bag.

"We assumed you'd show up on your lunch hour, so we packed you a peanut-butter-and-jelly sandwich," he said.

"Here, Mom." Becca handed it through the window.

A surprised smile lit her eyes. "Thank you. I thought I wouldn't get lunch today."

"No problem." He was pleased she seemed touched by the gesture.

Once she'd praised each child and thanked them for lunch, she drove away.

To Mark's amazement, the five of them finished the fence that afternoon. So he called it quits and took them inside to get cleaned up. Most of the paint came off, although splatters lingered in their hair.

He tugged on a bit of Becca's hair. "I hope your mom doesn't put me in the doghouse over the streaks of white."

"Whenever we make a mess, she just says, 'It'll wash.'"

He wasn't so sure about the pile of dirty clothes. Of course, Becca had come out with another identical pink outfit. Come to think of it, pink was all she ever wore.

"You must love pink," he said.

"I do. It helps me remember my daddy."

"How so?"

She looked at him shyly and tugged at the hem of her shirt. "He always told me I looked pretty in pink."

Like a punch to the solar plexus, her announcement knocked the breath out of him, leaving him aching for Becca and the other kids. They'd lost so much. Hannah, too.

He wanted to do anything he could to ease the pain. To watch out for them.

And anything he could to lighten Hannah's load.

"Your daddy knew what he was talking about. You do look pretty in pink."

She grinned at him. "Thank you."

Encouraged by the fact he might be doing okay

with the kids, he decided to take one more risk. "So, let's take a vote. Do you want to rest and relax after working so hard? Or do you want to cook dinner for your mom?"

Every single one chose to cook. Even the boys. And since they'd cooperated so well painting, he assigned them challenging jobs.

Determination lit their eyes as they took to their tasks. With any luck at all, Hannah would come home to a nice, relaxing, tasty dinner.

Chapter Six

Paint streaked Hannah's children's hair and mingled with flour and something shiny and sticky on their faces. Maybe honey?

Blue lapped something off the floor, and doggie footprints that looked suspiciously like flour made wandering trails all over the kitchen.

The blender sat on the counter with something pink dripping down the sides and onto the counter. Dirty pots and baking sheets filled the sink.

Total disaster was the only way to describe the kitchen—if Hannah could utter a word. But shock glued her mouth shut.

"Hey, Mom's home!" Becca ran over and tried to push Hannah out of the kitchen. "Don't look yet. We'll call you when it's ready."

As the shock began to fade, Hannah zoomed in on the bandage wrapped around Becca's finger. "What happened?"

She shoved it behind her back. "Nothing. Please go wait in the family room."

"You're hurt." She reached for the hand.

But Tony grabbed her and tried to pull her out of the room. "You're ruining our surprise."

Hannah looked over at a harried Mark. "You said you'd call if there was blood. Did Becca cut herself?"

"Yes, while chopping the salad ingredients. But it stopped bleeding quickly. She's a real trouper." He winked at Becca.

Eric and Emily joined in the effort to push Hannah out, so she left them to the mess that was, apparently, dinner. By the time she'd changed, they were calling her to come and eat.

The four kids jumped up and down as she joined them in the kitchen.

"Dinner's ready," Mark said, his voice low and tired. She could see the anxiety in his eyes as his gaze darted around the room.

But despite the mess and Mark's apparent dread, the kids were in total bliss, with rosy faces from the sun and kitchen heat, big grins and bright eyes.

"We made dinner for you," Tony said, as proud as she'd ever seen him. He ran to the table and pulled out her chair for her.

Mark gave him a thumbs-up.

Refusing to say a word about the mess, she

took her seat. She could only hope that no matter how disastrous the place looked, Mark had spent enough time with the children that he couldn't bear to force them out of Redd's house.

Becca shoved a big bowl of salad at her while Emily passed a bread basket holding brown-and-serve rolls.

"Wow. You've worked hard today. Painting, and now this." She put her napkin in her lap. "Thank you."

"Okay, guys. Go ahead and join your mom. You did a great job."

They launched into their seats as if the wait had wound them as tightly as a spring. After a quick blessing—that Mark reminded them to say—they dug into mashed potatoes and gravy. Breaded pork chops lay on a platter across the table, and Emily and Eric each stabbed one with a fork to serve themselves.

"Did you really make all this from scratch?"

Becca pushed up her glasses and nodded. "Mark helped us."

"Looks like Blue helped, as well." When the kids gave her a questioning look, she pointed to the doggie prints on the floor.

Emily giggled. "He didn't steal anything."

Seeing her children happy and engaged warmed her more than the home-cooked meal.

As she scooped out potatoes, she noticed Mark

swiping at something on the counter. "Aren't you going to join us?" Surely he would stay to enjoy the fruits of his labor.

What terrible timing. Hannah had arrived home a half hour earlier than he'd expected. She didn't seem angry about the chaotic kitchen, but he couldn't be certain. "I need to jump on this mess. I had planned to have it cleaned up before you got here. But, well...you know how it is with good intentions."

She looked at him then, her green eyes giving nothing away. "Yes, I do."

He hurried into motion, rinsing the fruit smoothie from their afternoon snack out of the blender.

"Leave it," she said. "We'll all pitch in and have the place spotless in no time."

Becca jumped up and pulled out his chair. "Yeah, Mr. Mark. You have to taste everything you made."

He'd assumed Hannah would want to hurry him out the door. He could understand that. He'd shown up unexpectedly that day and had probably taken too many liberties. How many babysitters enlisted kids this age to cook a full meal and handed them knives?

But no, she smiled at him, encouraging, then glanced away shyly.

How could he not react to that sweet smile,

to the invitation to be with her family another night? "I don't see how I can resist pork chops and mashed potatoes."

"Well, then, that's settled." Hannah stared at her plate as if it was the most interesting thing in the world. As she pushed her silky black hair behind her ear, he thought he spied a smile.

His heart squeezed in his chest, causing an ache so acute he worried for his health. The woman could send his EKG off the charts with one simple smile.

"Dig in," he said as he stabbed a chop and put it on his plate.

Despite the gorgeous, alluring woman sitting across from him, he managed to wolf down a complete meal—that was pretty good, if he did say so himself.

As she predicted, they knocked out the cleanup job in no time.

"Kids, I'll guess I'll either see you tomorrow or at church on Sunday."

They told him goodbye, then thanked him after Hannah prompted them. As he walked out the front door, he heard footsteps behind him.

A few seconds later, Hannah followed him outside. "Thank you for filling in today."

She remained on the front porch. He stood on the ground at the bottom of the steps. "Sorry about the mess in the kitchen. And that you'll probably be getting stuff out of their hair for a week."

Her expression wasn't happy, but she didn't look angry, either. Yet something was definitely wrong.

As if all the energy had gone out of her, she plunked down to the top step. "No worries. It'll wash."

He couldn't resist smiling because Becca knew her mom so well. "Then what's got you distressed?"

She was nearly on eye level now. Evening sunlight gave a warm glow to her skin and shiny hair. "I find that your kindness has put me in a predicament."

He joined her on the stairs, making sure not to crowd her, not to touch his shoulder to hers. "I'm sorry."

"My mother is very upset that you've come home, as I'm sure you've noticed."

His quiet huff of laughter punctuated the air. "I noticed."

"I'm sure she'll hear about today from the kids. And about dinner last night...and tonight. She won't be happy."

"Look, I can come and fix up the house and try to stay away from you and the kids. I don't want to cause trouble." Even as he said it, a bit of the old emptiness gnawed on him. He honestly didn't want to be forced to stay away. How could he ever make up for what he'd done if he couldn't get near Hannah?

She sighed. "Tony seemed really happy for the first time in ages. And I have you to thank." She cut her eyes toward his, but looked away quickly. "I guess if you keep working on the house, it shouldn't be too hard to go our own way while you go yours."

"Today, my dad seemed more receptive to me doing repairs around here. So if I don't have to worry about his schedule, I can try to work around yours. No big deal."

But it was a big deal. He'd thought maybe he'd found a way to make up for the past by helping Hannah's family. Now, even that opportunity had been taken away.

Not to mention that for the first time in years, he'd had a taste of what it felt like to be part of a family.

And had maybe started to care?

He got up and walked to his car, sick at heart. He'd have to stay away from Hannah and her children. He didn't want her paying for letting him into her home.

Mark honored Hannah's wishes and stayed away on Saturday, helping Ann around her house and yard. He'd decided not to push his luck with his dad. Would lie low, hoping brief moments with

Redd as he worked around the house would heal the rift.

Lord, thank You that Dad's coming around. I know that's Your work.

That morning, as he escorted Ann to church, they walked past the back section of the church where Hannah and her family filled the pew. He didn't risk a glance in their direction, but kept his eyes forward. Yet he knew she had seen him, could somehow sense it. Only massive willpower kept him from looking.

As he followed Ann into her regular pew, she stopped him. "Go on down and sit with your daddy."

"I don't think that's wise." He glanced at his dad's back and knew he didn't want to attempt it.

"I think if you just march right up there and don't give him a choice, then it'll eventually work out."

He laughed, catching the attention of a few people around them. Her suggestion went totally against his plan, but then again, not much of his plan had worked so far. Maybe he should trust Ann's instincts. "Okay. If I end up humiliated, it's your fault."

"I'll be praying for you both." As she patted his arm, her face crinkled up in a big smile. Her warm touch was surprisingly reassuring, giving him the gumption to proceed.

When he got to Redd's row, instead of leaning in and asking if he could join him, Mark sat right down beside him, as if it were something he did every Sunday. He gave his dad a brief nod of greeting and then opened his bulletin and started flipping through it.

Redd didn't say a word. Didn't move a muscle. Didn't even acknowledge his son's presence.

But he didn't boot Mark out into the aisle, either. Probably a good sign.

At least now he could make progress on the house. But what for? To move his dad back in? That meant kicking Hannah out. Something he now realized he couldn't do.

The time had come to rethink his goal. Would it be so bad for Redd to live in the garage for a couple of years? He seemed happy there. Seemed to like having a family around. Maybe the living arrangement was good for everyone involved. Mark could even come back during a future vacation to refurbish the garage.

Mark pulled his attention back to worship. Throughout the rest of the service, he and his dad sat side by side without even looking at each other. Six inches, yet miles apart.

Once it was over, Mark turned to him. "Thanks for letting me join you."

His dad nodded silently. When Redd didn't

make any overture to having a meal together, Mark excused himself and left the pew to meet up with Ann.

"Looks promising," she said.

"He didn't run off screaming." He took her arm and placed it snugly in the crook of his, then smiled at his friend, actually feeling happy. Happy and hopeful.

Lord, help us get out of here without a confrontation.

Hannah breathed easier, if not easily, as she, her children and Donna left the service. Another few minutes and they'd escape without running into Mark. Without her mother making a scene.

As they came down the front steps of the church, Gabe flagged her down. "Hey, can I talk to you for a second?"

She asked her mom to take the kids to the car. "Sure."

Gabe, wearing street clothes instead of his uniform now that he took Sundays off to attend church with his daughter and Faith, hurried to catch up with her. "In planning the youth group's upcoming Appalachian mission trip, we've realized we have two or three kids who won't be able to afford to go. So I told Phil we'd do a couple of fundraisers."

He hadn't sugarcoated the facts. And she could tell where this was leading. "And you want my help."

"You're the money expert."

Some expert—she barely made ends meet. She gave him a crooked smile. "I only work at the bank. I don't have access to the money, you know."

"But you know a lot of folks around town. You deal with a lot of the businesses. Could you possibly help us round up a few donors? Maybe help find sponsors for three of the youths?"

"Is this similar to the trip last year?"

"Yes. We're going to Appalachia to repair homes to prevent them from being condemned."

Since Gabe had grown up in Corinthia, he knew her past—that she and her mom had lost their home and briefly lived in a shelter. Everyone around knew that she had a soft spot for the homeless. All Gabe had to do was mention it and she was on board.

Maybe finding three sponsors wouldn't be difficult or take much time. "You know I'll help any way I can."

"Thanks."

"Gabe," Faith hollered from beside the church with a worried expression, waving him over. "We need you back here." She nodded at Hannah. "You might want to come, too."

Gabe took off at full speed. He didn't have his weapon on him, as far as she could tell. Though totally irrational, visions of robberies and kidnappings sent her heart into overdrive.

She took off after him.

When she rounded the church and reached the back parking lot, she found a crowd gathered near what looked like Mark's rental car. Her heart plummeted when she spotted her mom raging at him—and her kids nowhere to be found.

As soon as she pushed through the crowd, Mark looked over.

"The kids are inside the church with Ann," he said, apparently wanting to put her at ease.

"I told you to stay away from my family," Donna spat. "My grandkids told me you put them to work painting. That's gotta be against some kind of child labor laws or something."

"Now, Donna…" Gabe said, trying to get in between the two of them.

Hannah inserted herself in the fray. "Mom, that's enough!"

She turned her full ire on Hannah. "You should be thanking me for getting him away from your kids."

"He was just being helpful while you were sick."

"Helpful my eye." She jabbed a finger in Mark's chest. "Go back where you belong. We don't want you around here."

"Come on." Gabe took Donna's hand and led her away, toward her house.

Hannah could tell he was talking to her, trying to calm her, as they went.

Looking around at the appalled faces, Hannah wanted to crawl inside her car and slink away. Instead, she said, "Okay, folks. Show's over."

Faith helped direct people away, leaving only Mark beside his rental car. He let out a deep gush of air. "Thanks for rescuing me."

"Thanks for letting me know where the kids are. Did they see any of my mom's theatrics?"

"No. I saw her heading at me, looking like a geyser ready to blow, and I asked Ann to hurry them inside."

Why couldn't the children's own grandmother have thought about their welfare? "I'm sorry. She doesn't let go of a grudge, and she lets it blind her to everything and everyone around her." Like she had Hannah's whole life, making her feel invisible while Donna worried over Sydney.

"Look, I know what I did was rotten. Like you said, your family fell apart. Sydney is still struggling. Your mom has every right to be angry."

"Well, she has no right to accost you in the church parking lot."

He gave her a sweet smile that did funny things to her stomach and for some reason made her want to burst into tears. This was Mark Ryker. She shouldn't feel bad for him. Yet the past few days made it difficult to think like Donna. God wouldn't want her to hold on to the past.

He nodded toward the church. "Come on, let's go get them. From here on out, I'll stay away from your mom."

He truly did seem to have changed. In high school, he was cocky and rebellious. Couldn't Donna see the difference? The man had changed his life, was once again attending church. And now he didn't feel welcome even here.

"No, you can't let her stop you from coming to church. We'll use the front door. You use the back door."

The laugh that came out of him didn't jibe at all with the anguish on his face. "I know I should probably head back to Seattle. But with Dad starting to warm up, I can't. I'll do my best not to turn your life upside down."

This time tears popped into her eyes.

As he held the door open for her, he noticed them. "Hey, don't be upset. It'll be okay."

How could she tell him she wasn't upset over her mother? She simply didn't want to see him hurt.

And that was plain crazy. Why this sudden softness for the man who'd destroyed her family?

Maybe God was already healing old hurts.

"Mommy!" Emily ran over, followed closely by Eric.

"Mr. Mark!" Tony called as he and Becca joined the stampeding children.

Ann looked over at Mark, concerned. "Are we ready to go?"

"Everything's fine," he said. "Time to head home for lunch."

But everything wasn't fine. This man, who for all intents and purposes wanted to run Hannah out of her house, had somehow edged his way into her life.

And Donna would make everyone miserable if Hannah allowed him in.

Chapter Seven

A burst of irritation flashed behind Mark's eyes Monday morning as he adjusted his schedule to fit Donna's order to avoid her family, waiting until he was sure Hannah had left for the bank before heading to the house. But the irritation quickly diverted. To himself. Because he couldn't get Hannah out of his mind.

Her gorgeous green eyes haunted his dreams. She was a good woman. A good mother. He enjoyed her company. When he woke up that morning, the first thing he wanted was to see her and the kids.

But she was off-limits. Unless he could think of some way to convince Donna otherwise...

Forget it. Donna wasn't the forgiving type. No way Hannah would be interested anyway.

Hand on the steering wheel, he mashed the gas pedal and headed to his dad's property. The whole issue was a moot point anyway. His life was three thousand miles away.

When he pulled up to the house, he discovered Hannah's van. The kids stood on the porch and raced out to his car when they saw him.

Uh-oh. A problem with Donna?

"Did you come to watch us?" Becca asked as she pushed up her glasses.

"Sorry, but I'm here to do repairs."

The front door closed, pulling his attention away from the kids. Hannah froze when she saw him. Awareness sparked between them. Then a smile lit her face.

Could Hannah Hughes be happy to see him?

She'd been wary, tentative with him before. Antagonistic, even. This smile gave him a jolt. *No way.* No way could there be attraction between the two of them.

And if there was…well, he couldn't allow it.

As her long, shapely legs carried her toward the car, black hair swirling around her face, fitted suit accenting every curve, he couldn't take his eyes off her. *Definitely not a pesky kid anymore.*

Mouth dry as sawdust, he tried to swallow.

"Y'all hurry and get in the van. We're late."

They ran and climbed in as she searched her bag for keys. "I'm late. My mom called this morning and said she couldn't take them until nine-thirty. I think she's trying to punish me."

His earlier irritation ballooned into full-blown anger. Why would a woman want to make her own daughter's life more difficult? "I'm sorry. Will it cause problems at the bank?"

She flashed the keys once she found them. "I hope not. I just took some personal leave time. But I hate doing it last minute like that."

"I can help anytime you need it. Maybe Donna wouldn't find out."

She returned his irreverent grin. "I have half a mind to take you up on it right this minute. Guess I'm not brave enough, though." She hurried to her side of the van and waved goodbye.

Mark had his projects planned for the day, but after rummaging through the tool shed discovered he needed to buy some supplies at his dad's store before he could begin. Might help him get on Redd's good side.

He hadn't yet told Hannah he'd decided there was no way he could move his dad back in the house anytime soon. He should probably make a quick trip to the bank to tell her. He should also thank her for keeping her promise not to tell Redd about the donation. So far so good in that department. And as long as his dad didn't mention the money, Mark wouldn't, either.

When he arrived at the hardware store, Redd was busy with a customer, so he began gathering the materials he needed—more sandpaper, more primer, a new wire brush. Mark knew exactly where every item was located, which was oddly reassuring—comforting even, that some things never changed.

He could depend on finding nuts and bolts on aisle two. Plumbing supplies on aisle four. Lawn and garden on aisle seven.

"Finding everything you need?" his dad asked from behind him as Mark bent down to grab a box of nails.

"Sure am. I'm glad you've left everything the same."

"Never had the urge to make the place all new-fangled. Why mess with a good thing?"

Yet, according to Phil, the business was struggling now. "I like knowing where everything is, and I imagine others feel the same."

"I did go to a computer system a few years ago. Didn't like it at first, but it's made things easier. I guess some things do have to change to keep up."

Yes, Mark had learned *he* had to change. With God's help.

"Holler if you need anything."

"Dad, wait. I wanted to talk to you if you have a second."

"I'm pretty busy. Time to send out billing."

Mark nodded. There wouldn't be any heart-to-hearts with Redd. "I know I've pressured you to move back in the house. But I realized you're right. Hannah and her kids need the house until they can build. So I won't push you anymore."

"Way I figure it, that's been my decision to make all along."

Touché.

"You're right. I shouldn't have presumed you might want my opinion." He grabbed another twelve-pack of shutter fasteners. He and his dad had made a smidgen of progress, so he tried not to let discouragement take over. "I've got a couple more items to pick up, then I'll be ready to check out."

He couldn't let his dad get under his skin. The man was obviously not going to all of a sudden pronounce forgiveness and reach out with open arms. Mark had to be patient. In the meantime, the house would end up in better condition.

After he bought the supplies, he headed to the car to drop off his purchases. Then he walked into the bank and headed toward the back, to Hannah's office.

Hannah's eyes widened when she saw him coming, and she glanced around, as if hoping no one spotted him approaching. He got the feeling he should have come incognito. More than sunglasses alone could handle.

She sat up perfectly straight. Tense. "What can I do for you, Mr. Ryker?"

Mr. Ryker? "I just stopped by to let you know

I'm not going to push my dad to move back into the house. He seems happy where he is and is enjoying having your family around."

She remained straight and still and didn't appear to breathe. "So you're okay with us being there for the next couple of years? Even if your dad is financially able to quit renting it out?"

"Yes."

Her shoulders relaxed a fraction. "Why?"

He hadn't anticipated her asking why. What could he say? *Because I have a totally inappropriate attraction to you and want you and your kids to be happy?* "Like I said, Dad's happy. You're happy. I should leave well enough alone."

She leaned back in her chair on an audible exhale. "Thank you. I appreciate your honesty."

No, she wouldn't have appreciated his total honesty. She'd probably have been freaked out by it. But the partial truth would suffice. "Gotta get back to the house. Need to finish the shutters."

"Feel free to work as late as you like. I'm not worried about incidental contact."

Incidental contact. Of course, she meant social contact. Yet he fought the urge to brush his palm over her soft cheek. To run his fingers through her hair to see if it was as silky as it had seemed when it skimmed his knuckles the other day.

He wanted to wrap her in his arms. To protect her. Help her with her children.

What was wrong with him? Never mind they lived at opposite ends of the country, and he had a company to run. The woman would never consider a relationship with him at the risk of alienating her mother.

He slammed his sunglasses on and stalked out before she saw the need she'd unleashed in him. The need to connect. To know her better.

Lord, I've been selfish all my life. Help me fight the temptation now. Keep reminding me that I hurt this woman years ago. Give me strength to fight wanting her in my life when I know that would only bring her grief.

When Hannah drove into the clearing, she saw him.

Mark.

He stood near the front porch, working over a sawhorse. Skin tanned. Golden hair gleaming in the sun.

When he heard them and looked up, she over-braked and jarred them all.

"Mom. The seat belt just locked," Becca griped.

"Sorry."

As Hannah got out of the car and approached, he dried his face with the edge of his T-shirt. He turned and met her with those penetrating feline eyes.

"Hi. I took you up on your offer to stay late. Almost finished with the sanding."

Words failed her. How could this man make her pulse jump? Make her wish for so much more in life?

Wish for things she couldn't have.

She nodded. Cleared her throat. "No problem." With extreme effort, she dragged her eyes away from him. "Kids, come inside and help with dinner."

"Can I stay out here and help?" Tony asked, his voice quiet and unsure.

Her gaze darted to Mark, and those wishes suddenly paled in comparison to the wish for him to be tender with her children.

Mark ruffled Tony's hair. "Fine with me if it's okay with your mom."

She sucked in air and resumed breathing. "Sure. Just be careful and do what he tells you to do."

Tony sidled over beside Mark. "I'm a good painter. Can I do that?"

"Well, buddy, I planned to paint the lower shutters with primer tomorrow if it doesn't rain. But you can help me finish the sanding." He squatted down and handed him some fine-grade sandpaper. "You got any protective goggles inside?"

"I have some for swimming."

"I imagine that'll do."

Tony grinned as he ran inside. The other three kids took off, following.

Though trying to guard herself from feelings for Mark, she couldn't ignore his kindness to Tony. "Thank you."

In less than a minute, Tony zoomed out the door looking like a goggle-eyed fish.

Mark gave a chuckle and showed him where to start.

Becca trailed behind in pink swim goggles, squinting without the aid of her glasses. "Can I help, too?"

Even though she wouldn't be able to see for detail work, he gave her a job anyway, showing her how to brush off the largest paint chips and debris from the last shutter.

When the twins showed up a couple of minutes later wearing matching green goggles, Mark burst out laughing and seemed to concede accomplishing much. "Come on, you two. Help me glue the shutter joints back together."

Eric and Emily's dark heads bent next to Mark's blond one as they watched him demonstrate. He held the bottle of wood glue as Emily applied it. He guided Eric's hands to press the wood together.

As the hot evening sun streamed across the yard heating Hannah's skin, warmth bathed her insides. Mark would be such a good dad someday. A good husband.

For some lucky woman.

She smiled encouragement at Tony, patted Becca's shoulder and dragged her gaze away from Mark and the twins. Dinner wouldn't make itself.

Once she had a pot of water boiling, she tossed in the macaroni. A salad would at least offer some vegetables, with a main course of mac and cheese. As she sliced a cucumber, she popped a piece in her mouth and chewed carefully.

She'd gnawed the inside of her cheek that afternoon at work after receiving an email from the branch administrator asking her to please give more notice when she was going to come in late. As if she had control of her child-care provider calling in sick at the last minute, or being delayed.

Add to that, Donna was still miffed about Mark spending time around Hannah and the kids. And when Donna stayed miffed, Hannah never knew what she might do.

With salad on the table, rolls in the oven and the main course on the stove keeping warm, she walked out to the front porch. A slight breeze lifted the hair from her shoulders, sending shivers down her arms.

She wanted to blame the wind, but suspected it was as much a reaction to the man working side by side with her children.

"You've accomplished a lot," she called. More than she'd expected.

Mark looked up, smiling, eyes shining. He seemed as happy as the kids. "We have. Another couple hours of work and I'll be ready to prime."

She motioned the children inside. "Y'all come and eat."

"Thanks for helping," he called as they zipped up the stairs.

"You're welcome, Mr. Mark," Becca called back.

Hannah crossed her arms loosely in front of her, pressing against her stomach, testing. It hadn't hurt in a couple of days. "You're really good with the kids."

"I'm good with repairs. Your kids are good around other people. You've raised them well."

His praise was balm for a struggling mom. Peace fell over her as he approached the porch.

He wiped his hands on his jeans. "You really have. They're well behaved and happy."

She stood at the top of the steps and tightened her arms around her waist. "I want to be everything to them, to provide all they need. Sometimes it just seems impossible."

He climbed steps, coming within inches of her. "You mean financially?"

"Financially, emotionally, spiritually..."

"Raising four kids is a lot of pressure for one

person. Maybe you should cut yourself some slack. Let others help you more."

She already depended on her mom beyond her comfort level. Besides, no amount of help from Donna would fund her dream. "I won't quit worrying until we're securely in our own home."

He gently cupped her upper arm and gave a light squeeze. "You'll do it."

His hands were warm and work-roughened. She wanted to pull away but couldn't resist his tender touch. As she tried to gather strength to move, he brushed his thumb back and forth on her arm and gave one last, encouraging squeeze.

She wanted to lean into him, to have him hold her and tell her she would have that security, would fill that missing piece in her life.

What then? Could owning a house really provide what she needed?

For the first time in years, she questioned everything she'd been striving for to make her feel secure.

Mark could.

No, she had to do this herself if she was going to find security for her family. Platitudes—and strong arms—wouldn't get her anywhere.

And if she gave in to the desire to allow him to be her rock? She couldn't do that. Though the relationship with her mother was sometimes bumpy, the woman had always done the best she could.

Had always protected Hannah and loved her. Donna would see a relationship with Mark as betrayal.

She took a step away from him.

But he was so good for her children. She couldn't turn the man away after he'd sacrificed his last working hour. "The kids would be thrilled if you'd stay to eat with us."

His mouth opened, poised to answer, yet no sound came out. He hung that way for a few seconds, as if weighing the decision.

The door opened, and Becca stuck her hand out, holding Hannah's cell phone. "Someone called."

"Thanks, sweetie." She glanced down, and saw the missed call was from Sydney. Her eyes darted to his. "My sister."

"Thanks for the invitation, but I should go and let you call her back."

"Yes, of course. I guess we'll see you tomorrow."

He walked down the steps, hands in his pockets, gaze trained on the ground. His steps seemed slow as he began to pack up his tools.

As she plodded inside to return Sydney's call, guilt nearly choked her. She'd been enjoying the touch of the man who had hurt her sister. She'd allowed her children to hang around him and to become attached.

What kind of sister was she?

She'd been lulled into thinking that time spent with Mark was innocent. Simple babysitting and repair work. Simple meals shared. She'd known if she let him into their lives, it would break the hearts of her family.

Yet she'd done it anyway.

Sometimes phone calls could be wake-up calls. He felt certain the call from Sydney that had interrupted them last night was a much-needed dash of reality. How could he hope to have a relationship with Hannah with their past between them? Besides, she'd never want to relocate them across the country.

He'd veered off track since arriving—enjoying time with Hannah and her family too much. Maybe God was trying to tell him something.

"Mark?" Ann tapped him on the arm. "Earth to Mark."

He pulled his mind off Hannah and back to Ann, his breakfast companion in the coffee shop. "Sorry. I was just wondering if I should head back to Seattle. A month is a long time to fill, and having me around is causing problems between Hannah and Donna."

She obviously knew Donna well, because she gave him a sympathetic smile. "I think your dad has enjoyed having you here."

He shook off the notion. "No. But he has warmed up to me a tad."

"I'm glad." Ann blew on her hot chocolate. "I'm also glad you joined me this morning."

He glanced at her Bible. "I don't want to keep you from your daily study."

"I'm in no hurry. I've enjoyed our time together."

He'd planned to go out to the house early before the predicted bad weather passed through, but decided to wait until everyone had left for work. Best to follow Donna's—and his dad's—wishes and stay away. He figured by now, the Hughes family would all be gone. He gulped the last of his coffee. "The sky's getting dark. I should go on to Dad's house. How about I cook dinner tonight?"

"You don't have to do that."

He stood and gave her a quick hug. "I know. It's my way of saying thank-you. And of impressing you with my culinary skills." He winked at her, then headed out the door onto the main street. He checked his phone for messages as he walked and didn't look up until he nearly ran into someone. "Oh, excuse—"

Redd, his face mottled red with rage, waved an envelope in Mark's face. "My bank statement came today. Care to tell me what you're up to?"

Mark glanced over at the hardware store and

noticed the sign that said Closed hanging on the door. Then he zoomed in on the envelope.

Great. "I'm not up to anything."

"Then how did a large sum of money get deposited into my account?"

"Maybe a donor wanted to help."

"Help an old man he thinks is a failure?"

"No, not at all. I'm sure the donor just wanted to tide you over until business picks up—once customers realize they miss the personalized service you offer."

Redd leaned in close and tapped the envelope against Mark's chest. "I don't want your charity. I don't want you stickin' your nose in my business."

Okay, so he couldn't try to deny he'd put the funds in his dad's account. Surely his dad would accept honesty. "I wanted you to be able to pay the back taxes so you wouldn't have to rent out our family home."

Something that looked like shame flashed across Redd's face. "You gave up the right to *our* family home when you hightailed it out of here and didn't look back. When you didn't call your mom. When—" A sob escaped before he cleared his throat. "When you didn't even keep in contact so we could let you know she'd died." The last words came out so quietly, Mark barely heard them.

Their eyes locked. So much could be said, but

he didn't know where to start. Apparently, nothing had changed between them. Discouragement—and the fact that he didn't want his dad to see the hurt—made him look away. "I'm sorry. For then. For now." He ran his hand through his hair and stared over at his dad's shop. At the courthouse. At the coffee shop. He didn't belong here. He belonged back in Seattle. In his office. Accomplishing something. "If you want me to leave town, I will."

Redd backed off. Shoved the envelope in his shirt pocket. Then began to pace up and down the sidewalk, staring at the ground ahead as if lost in thought.

Mark watched, unsure whether to say anything more. The fact that his dad hadn't immediately told him to leave gave a spark of hope.

After a long stroll up the sidewalk, he turned and came back, his face a picture of grief—eyes etched with sadness, a deep crease between the brows.

"Your mom would have my hide if I sent you away. She'd want us to make peace."

Swallowing was impossible, but he somehow managed to force air across his vocal cords. "I'd really like that, too."

The moment of reconciliation was broken by a car horn honking. Redd waved to the driver, then refocused on Mark. "But I won't accept your money. I take care of my property as I see fit."

"I hope you'll keep it and reconsider."

"If you won't go with me to the bank to get it out, I'll give it away." He brightened as if he'd had a stroke of genius. "Yessiree, I'll give it to charity."

"The money is yours to do with as you please." He just hoped his dad would make the smart choice. The practical choice.

"I don't want that money in my account another hour. Last chance to come with me to the bank."

Though he was glad his dad hadn't given him the boot out of town, he had to bite down on his frustration. "Think I'll pass. I plan to go prime the shutters if the storm will hold off."

"Suit yourself." He strode away. A man on a mission.

A mission to reject Mark's offer of help.

Thunder rumbled in the distance, and as he looked up, a drop of rain smacked him in the eye. "Perfect. Just perfect."

Mark headed to his car and ignored the vibrating cell phone in his pocket. Whoever was calling could wait.

Chapter Eight

"Come on," Hannah begged. She pulled the phone away from her ear and shouted at the receiver, "Answer your phone!"

All she'd wanted to do was put Mark out of her mind, go to work, do her job and make a living so she could support her family. But no. Donna had to go off the deep end and blackmail her own daughter.

Apparently, my warnings to stay away from Mark didn't work. That man is a danger to you. So I'm calling to tell you I won't be babysitting again until you convince him to leave town.

She'd wanted to shout at her mother that her devious plan had backfired. Now Hannah would be forced to call him and ask another favor. But instead, she'd bitten her tongue and counted to ten.

Becca walked into the room and stared up at her mother, her face scrunched in a frown, as if she thought Hannah was crazy. "Who are you yelling at?"

"Oh, no one. I'm just frustrated that Mark isn't answering his phone."

"Is Nana sick again?"

She couldn't lie to her children, but how could she explain that even though their grandmother had good intentions, her behavior was immature, selfish and stubborn? "Nana just can't watch you today." *Won't, more like it.*

"Did you try Miss Ann?"

"She's not home. I imagine she's over at the coffee shop." And Hannah was already late for work. Again. "I wonder if Chelsea Reynolds is old enough to babysit."

Frustration boiled over into anger. How could her own mother let spite put Hannah's job—her livelihood, the welfare of her family—at risk?

"Come on, kids. I'll have to take you with me to work and see if I can find someone in town to watch you."

By the time she got them all buckled in, drove in the spitting rain and arrived at the bank, she was twenty minutes late. The head teller eyed her, then resumed her phone conversation. Amy looked as if she knew trouble was brewing.

"Okay, you four, I need you to sit here and be on your best behavior." She pointed to the grouping of couches not far from her office. "I'll find someone to watch you. In the meantime, Mommy needs you to be patient. Okay?"

"Hannah." Amy touched her forearm. "I'm sorry to bother you, but Mr. Ryker has been in your office for—"

Oh, please... "Mark Ryker?"

"No, Redd. He's been insisting on seeing you. Has been here since we opened. And..." Her nose wrinkled.

"Yes?"

"Cheryl called. She wants you to call as soon as you get in."

Hannah's heart plummeted. Her boss knew she was late again. *Lord, please help her to be understanding.* "Thanks, Amy. I'm sorry I'm late. And had to bring the gang."

"No problem." The look she gave was sympathetic.

Hannah hurried to her office. "Hi, Redd. What can I do for you?"

"I want Mark's money gone." He jammed his hands into his pockets, a far cry from his son's country-club pose. Redd's posture shouted determination. "I want to give it to the church. In fact, how about to the youth? I could sponsor a bunch more kids now."

Oh, no. Poor Mark.

She nearly gasped when she realized that her first thought had been for Mark. What was wrong with her? She should be thrilled that all her fund-raising for the mission trip could be accomplished if she simply accepted the offer. "Well…yes…you could." The words dragged out of her as if her heart had overtaken her mouth.

His brows drew downward. "Well, do you want the money or not?"

"How will Mark feel about that?"

With brows still drawn, his eyes squinted, probing. "Why would you care how Mark feels?"

Busying herself with a stack of papers on her desk, she focused on anything other than the man who'd discovered something she hadn't wanted to broadcast.

She cared how Mark felt. Didn't want him hurt. Not good.

With one last pat to the pile of papers, she moved around behind her desk and sat. She braved looking him in the eye. "The church would be thrilled with a donation to the youth mission trip. Thank you for your generosity."

He pulled a bank statement out of his pocket. Then he took out his checkbook and scratched out a check for the full amount Mark had deposited. He ripped it out with a flourish and handed it to her. "There. I'm rid of that guilt offering."

Though the check would do much good, it pained her. "I'm sorry the two of you aren't on better terms. Can't you forgive him?"

He glanced away, his eyes unfocused, and Hannah had the feeling he was gazing into the past. "He broke his mother's heart. An apology can't fix that."

Nearly the exact words she'd said to Mark that night in the garden at the inn. She jerked back in her chair, stunned. She'd been as unforgiving as Redd. "I guess it can't fix anything in the past. But it could help you move forward."

Like she could move forward. She had the opportunity to extend the hand of forgiveness…to the detriment of her relationship with her mother, and the relationship between the children and their grandmother.

Could she take such a risk?

Redd stood and offered his hand. "Thank you for taking care of this donation. I hope every child will get to go on the mission trip."

"They certainly will."

When they walked out of her office, her kids rushed over to hug him.

"What are y'all doing here with your mom?"

Tony, whose mood had matched the gloomy weather all morning, said, "Nana didn't want to keep us today."

Redd's eyes darted to Hannah's at the same moment Tony's words knifed her heart. "No, sweetie. She just…well, she *couldn't* do it today."

"Did you try Ann?"

"Yes. No answer."

"Probably at the café." He sighed. "I know it'd make Donna mad as a hornet. Not too fond of the idea myself. But call Mark. He won't be able to paint with the storm moving this way."

"Thanks for the suggestion." She saw Redd out the door. Yes, she would call Mark. Again. And maybe he'd answer this time.

But first, she had to call her boss.

She located paper and pens and set the kids to drawing, then dialed her supervisor. "Hi, Cheryl. I was with a customer and just got a second to return your call."

"Hannah, we certainly trust you and know you're a hard worker. But I need to know you're capable of—and dedicated to—your role as branch manager there in Corinthia."

Heat flamed up her neck and across her cheeks. "Definitely. I've had some problems with my summer child-care provider, but I promise you I'll find a solution."

"See that you do. I'd hate to have to bring in someone else to take over as manager."

"Thanks for your patience. That won't be necessary." They hung up, and Hannah fought the urge to call her mother and give her an earful. Venting wouldn't help matters, though. Besides, Donna had been doing her a favor by babysitting at no charge. Hannah really couldn't complain.

Maybe it was time she hired someone to watch her children. The expense would further delay buying a house, but she'd keep her job.

She jotted a note on her calendar to call the child-care center as soon as she could. Then she tried one last time to reach Mark.

"Hey. Sorry I missed your call earlier. Dad and I had a bit of a run-in, so I couldn't pick up."

She let out a pent-up breath. The rich, deep tone of his voice made the muscles in her shoulders let go of their tight hold. She smiled, even though her mother had left her in a jam and her boss had threatened to take away her promotion. "I'm so glad you answered. Is there any way you could possibly watch the kids for me today?"

"Your mother giving you grief again? Over me?"

"Yep. So do you feel guilty enough to babysit?"

He snorted a laugh. "I'm a pro at guilt. I may as well make up for it where I can."

"Thank you. I'll bring them to the house right now."

"I'll be waiting."

His words sent shock waves through her, creating visions of him waiting for her in *their* home.

She was acting like an indecisive teenager—one minute vowing to stay away from him, the next, thankful for the excuse to call him.

Her mother refused to babysit until he left town.

He was the only person who could do the job at the moment. A vicious cycle that could only be broken when she convinced him to leave.

But how could she do that when time with him was so limited? When she wanted nothing more than to spend every last minute with him?

Mark stood on Hannah's front porch staring through the rain at the darkening southwestern sky. He'd heard about a cold front coming through, but didn't think the predicted storms would be severe. The challenge would be entertaining the kids all day inside.

Maybe if he put in a movie he could do some interior work.

Hannah's van splashed up the muddy driveway. Blue came out from under the porch and ran along beside them. The children threw the doors of the vehicle open, calling to Blue as well as Mark. Felt pretty good to know he ranked up there with a beloved dog.

Blue spotted Mark on the porch and barreled up, wagging his tail and sniffing Mark's hands. Without warning, the black Lab shook from head to tail, spraying water all over Mark even as he tried to duck away from the shower. "Good to see you, too, buddy."

While Hannah popped up an umbrella to make the short walk to the door, the kids ran ahead.

Becca and the twins threw their arms around him in greeting.

"You're going to watch us today?" Tony did a quick-release hug, a big deal for him.

Eight small arms had made him feel more welcome than...well, than anything ever had. He coughed into his hand. "Sure am. Why don't you all head inside? I'll be there after I talk to your mom."

As soon as the front door opened and then closed, peace descended.

Rain pattered on the roof of the porch. Thunder echoed in the distance. Hannah stood close, smelling like rain and flowers, tempting him with her nearness.

"Thank you for watching them. I hope they won't be any trouble."

"I told you, they're good kids. We'll be fine."

She nodded, glanced at the darkening sky. "Your dad came in this morning to withdraw your money." She reached out and touched his arm, her eyes full of sympathy. "I'm sorry. I know you only wanted to help him."

"Yeah, well..." He, too, checked out the rapidly moving clouds. "I may be leaving town soon. My plan isn't working."

"You should talk to him. I mean really talk. About the past. About how you both feel now."

"Look, I've done all I can. I tried to help him pay the taxes. I'm doing repair work on the house."

"Have you done repair work on the father-son relationship? He needs to know you're going to stick around for more than a few thousand dollars and a gallon of paint."

"Ouch." Blunt but honest. He liked that.

Her nose crinkled as she winced. "I'm sorry. I probably speak my mind more than I should. I've learned the hard way I need to count to ten before I speak."

"No counting necessary with me."

A slow smile lifted her rosy lips. She leaned closer. "So...will you talk to him?"

When she looked at him like that, her bright eyes so earnest, how could he refuse? "I guess it can't hurt."

"Good." She reached for her umbrella. "I should go."

"Any interior projects that you need done?"

She stepped under her umbrella and into the rain. "Just the nurturing of four young, impressionable children." She looked back over her shoulder, a playful sparkle in her eyes. "No biggie."

Scary, intimidating business. "Sounds like my most important project ever."

She smiled a ray of sweet light, brightening the dreary day. "And you better not forget it."

Grinning, he went in search of the gang. "Okay,

who's going to help me find a repair project to do inside today?"

Emily came dashing down the stairs. "You can clean my room."

A laugh burst out before he could stop it. He knelt and gave her a serious look. "I think we need to do something for your mom. Do you know of anything she's talked about doing but hasn't had a chance to get to?"

Trying to look grown-up, Emily tapped her chin in thought. "Hmm…"

"We can teach Blue to sit and stay," Eric said, his shoulders proudly thrust back. "She's always saying that's our next big project."

"Not a bad idea. How about something with the house itself, though?"

Tony tapped him on the shoulder. "The rocking chairs on the front porch."

The chairs his mom and dad had loved so much. He could remember hearing them out there, sitting together each night after he and Matt went to bed. Laughing. Talking politics. And, yes, sometimes arguing. But they always settled their differences before they came back inside. "You know what? That's a great idea. We can do the prep work out there on the porch."

Pleased with himself, Tony bit his lip, as if trying not to smile too big. "Can I do the paint?"

"You sure can, once we get to that. For today, let's sand off the old paint and fix any loose slats."

"Yay!" Becca jumped up and down like a little cheerleader. "Then I'll be able to sit out there and read without getting splinters."

They all dug in and helped, working the morning away. The chairs would be ready to prime once the humidity dropped. "I imagine you're all getting hungry. How about—"

"Mr. Mark, it looks weird out here." Becca pushed up her glasses and stared out into the yard.

Intent on overseeing their work, Mark hadn't noticed that the wind had kicked up, and the sky had taken on an eerie green cast.

"I don't like the look of that sky. Let's go inside and check the weather report."

Emily grabbed his hand, her dark brown eyes wide with terror.

He had to remember he was dealing with children and quit speaking the first thing that popped into his mind. "It's okay. I'm here to take care of you."

She nodded, but her small hand tightened. "I want my mommy," she whispered.

Eric stuck his tongue out at his sister and nearly sneered. "Nah, nah, nah, nah. She's scared of storms."

"Be nice to your sister." The wind picked up, kicking leaves and debris around the yard. A low, heavy cloud moved steadily across the sky, bringing even more green darkness. "Inside. Now."

He tried not to let his tension show as he turned on the television to a local network. A storm report had preempted other shows and the weatherman was pointing to a map of north Georgia.

Their county was under a tornado warning.

He had to protect Hannah's kids.

His cell phone started buzzing, and he felt sure it was her. No time. He'd call her once they were safely...

Where? The house didn't have a basement.

"Why's that man telling people in Corinthia to seek shelter? What does that mean?" Becca asked.

"Let's play a little game and do what he's saying." He smiled to reassure Emily.

Tony didn't buy it. "What's going on?"

"We're going to play sardines and see if we can all squeeze in the little bathroom under the stairs. Come on!" He herded them ahead of him.

When they got to the powder room, the house began to creak as if the wind was trying to pull it apart. Somewhere, a window shattered. "Get in the corner by the sink. Now."

They didn't move fast enough to suit him, so he grabbed them in his arms and shoved them as a unit into the cramped space, covering them with his body. Emily's scream pierced his brain as the proverbial freight train roared by.

Then silence, punctuated with Emily's sobs. The storm was over as quickly as it had hit.

Grateful the kids were still bundled in his arms, he looked around. The walls were standing. A ceiling remained over their head. They even had power.

Emily whimpered.

"It's okay, Emily. Mark is here," Tony said, his green eyes wide and frightened.

Mark dared to breathe again. Weak with relief, he closed his eyes and thanked God for their safety. "Everyone okay?"

"What happened?" Becca tried to wiggle loose to straighten her glasses.

It was a wonder they hadn't been injured from him squeezing them so tightly. "That was a tornado, and it must have passed fairly close. Let's go call your mom and my dad. Check the damage."

Lord, please let Hannah and Dad be okay.

"She'll be worried," Tony said.

As they filed outside, Mark took out his cell phone, his heart pounding in fear. What if the downtown area took a direct hit?

No need to dial. The green minivan came barreling down the driveway doing about ninety, fishtailing in the water and mud. As he waved to let her know they were okay, his knees nearly went weak with relief.

Hannah slammed on her brakes and flung open

the door. She ran around the front of the van, then, when she saw them, stopped. Sobs poured out of her. Gut-wrenching sobs that seemed to rip his heart out of his chest.

The kids tore across the yard, and she gathered them in her arms, a couple of them joining her in the crying.

Not wanting to intrude on their reunion, he waited until the tears stopped. Once she let go of the kids, he strode over to join them. An onslaught of chatter greeted him as each child told a portion of the story.

"I wanted to cry."

"Mr. Mark shoved us in the corner."

"And he piled on top of us right when this really loud noise hurt my ears."

"I cried."

"Mom! A tornado! There was a real *tornado!*"

Emily raised her hand and waved it. "Mommy, did you hear me? I cried."

"Oh, sweetie, I'm so sorry you were scared and cried." Hannah hugged them all within her arms. She looked up, thanking him with her eyes. "The downtown area was spared. But I had to come make sure y'all weren't hurt."

Mark looked around. The house had withstood the tornado. Just some missing shingles and a couple of broken windows. Several trees down— thankfully not the huge live oak next to the house.

Branches littered the yard. Out beyond the pasture, a swath of flattened trees showed the path of the tornado. Too close for comfort. "Looks like only minor damage here."

"Thank You, God." Hannah sent the kids inside with the promise of joining them soon. She wiped her eyes and sniffed.

Mark shoved his hands in his pockets so he wouldn't embarrass himself by grabbing her. He wanted to pull her into his arms, kiss her tear-stained face. "You okay?"

"I am now."

"I'm sorry I couldn't answer your call. The storm came up so quickly, I—"

"No, don't be sorry. You took care of my babies, and I—" She swallowed as tears filled her eyes. Then she launched to her tiptoes and threw her arms around his neck. "I can't thank you enough."

He wrapped his arms around her waist, treasuring the opportunity to hold her close. But he didn't dare kiss her like he wanted. "I'm just glad you're okay." He closed his eyes. Everything was more than okay with her in his arms.

"I was so scared."

When she lowered to her flat feet and let go of his neck, he gently pressed her head to his chest, rested his cheek on the top of her head. "I was worried about you."

She relaxed into him and placed her hand on

his chest. "Oh, Mark, we can't have this. We don't have a chance of a future. I can't grow to depend on you."

"I know. This is crazy. Especially when my life is three thousand miles away." He breathed in the fresh, citrusy fragrance of her hair, committing it to memory. Nothing about the two of them together made sense. Unless it was God's doing. If so, how could they fix the impasse between him and Donna? Because he couldn't continue driving a wedge between Hannah and her mother.

He let go and stepped away from her. But not before one last touch of her hair.

He had to leave, had to head back to Seattle before he harmed the Williams family more than he already had. He'd take with him the memory of Hannah in his arms, of her silk, soft hair against his cheek and her sweet-smelling skin.

Of her sweet spirit and precious children.

He had to get away from her and try to clear his head. Grabbing his cell phone, he excused himself to check on his dad and Ann.

He had to remember Hannah Hughes was off-limits.

Maybe the conversations he needed to have with his dad could be done that night. He could even invite Redd out for a visit. Either way, Mark needed to leave town so he didn't cause Hannah any more trouble.

* * *

Hannah called the bank to let them know her children needed her and that she wouldn't be in the rest of the day. Since apparently someone at the branch had to have been reporting her tardiness, she called her supervisor. Cheryl understood, since the tornado had also touched down near the main office.

Hannah rounded up the kids and drove into town to check in with her mother. She knew the duplex hadn't been hit, because she'd passed it on the way out to her house. But the property had sustained some damage. When they arrived at the complex, they found Donna talking to her neighbor, who'd had a tree fall on her roof. The tree lay across the corner of the house, exposing part of the attic. Insulation lay strewn all around.

Donna waved them over. "I've been trying to call, but phone lines must be down. Is everyone okay?" She checked each child as he or she walked up, rubbing her hands over faces and arms to examine for injuries.

"They're fine. The house is fine except for some shingles, windows and downed trees."

"I haven't heard of any injuries, thank the good Lord. But the Hernes had their roof torn off. I'm collecting food and supplies to help."

"Oh, Nana, we were so scared," Emily said,

causing the four of them to launch into the same tale they'd told her at the house.

Hannah should have warned them not to talk about it. Of course, that would have been requesting the impossible. So instead, she gritted her teeth and tried to smile, waiting for her mother's blowup.

But Donna surprised her. She didn't fuss at all. Just listened to her grandkids recount the story of Mark's bravery and how he had saved them, and answered with the occasional "Wow" and "You don't say."

Hannah was just starting to feel hope that maybe her mom would come around now that Mark had protected her grandchildren, when Donna asked the kids to run to her house to fetch a box of emergency supplies off the table. As they hurried away, that's when Hannah noticed the fury sparking in her eyes.

"You asked him to babysit. Against my wishes."

"You didn't leave me any choice. My supervisor has threatened to take away my promotion."

"You know how I feel about this. It's hurtful that you're associating with *those Rykers* who ruined our lives."

"Mom, please. Can't we move beyond it? Mark's a changed man. Sydney is doing better. And God wants us to forgive. I'm ready to do that."

Donna grabbed her by the arm and pulled her

away from an embarrassed neighbor who'd been pretending to ignore the conversation. "Forgiveness or no forgiveness, we have to remember who's hurt us before so we don't get hurt again. I can't stand by and watch him hurt you or the kids."

Tears burned her nose—tears of frustration. Helpless to reason with Donna, she wanted to scream. *One Mississippi...two Mississippi...* "I really appreciate all the help you've given me since Anthony died. And I really want the kids to stay with you. They need family—especially after the fright of today's storm."

With a hopeful look on her face, Donna nodded. "I agree. They do."

"But I can't be late for work each time you get upset with something I've done and refuse to babysit. I need to know right now that you'll be there for the kids tomorrow and the rest of this summer—whether or not Mark has been around. Or else I'll be forced to sign them up at the day-care center." Another expense she couldn't afford.

Donna's face crumpled, and she took a step back as if Hannah had slapped her. But then she threw back her shoulders and straightened her spine. "No. I won't be party to this path toward self-destruction." Despite the steel backbone, her voice wobbled. "I guess you should go ahead and contact the day-care center. Tell the kids I'll come visit them there and will see them at church."

Before Hannah could respond, Becca and Tony approached, carrying the box together.

"Here, Nana," Tony called.

A donation of food for her neighbors in need.

Donna would help everyone in town…except her own daughter when she needed it most.

Chapter Nine

Mark called to let his assistant know he was returning to work. But he couldn't fathom leaving Corinthia. Crazy, since his life was in Seattle.

His home. His business. His friends. His church.

But in a matter of a couple of weeks, he felt more at home with Hannah and her family than he ever had anywhere else.

He'd messed up her life, though. Had caused strife when he'd come to mend relationships. The least he could do before he left was make a quick drive through town to assess the damage. See what he could do to help.

Several houses had roof damage, so he stopped by the hardware store. The place was empty as he headed straight to the aisle with packages of tarpaulins. Seemed everyone had either gone to the warehouse store or hadn't yet gone into repair mode.

"You finding what you need?" His dad didn't

seem surprised to see him. Just stood at the end of the shelving with his arms crossed in front of him.

"Looks like most people need tarps at this point."

"I figured you'd be in here buying supplies to help someone."

Once the last tarp landed in his cart with a heavy thud, he wheeled it toward his dad until they were standing two feet apart. "I'm leaving. Heading to Atlanta tonight to see when I can catch a flight out."

The slightest flutter of eyelids showed a flash of response as Redd managed, otherwise, to look unperturbed. "Care to tell me why?"

Mark's instincts said to just tell him it's complicated and keep moving. But he'd come to town to find forgiveness. This was his last chance to try. To really talk, like Hannah had suggested. "Instead of making amends like I'd hoped, I'm causing more trouble."

"Says who?"

"Says Donna Williams. She's giving Hannah a rough time about me hanging around."

"Guess I'm not making you feel too welcome, either."

He shrugged, feeling like a kid. A kid once again in trouble with his dad. "Until I got here, I didn't realize the extent of the pain I left behind. I can't begin to make up for the havoc I've caused."

"I thought you said God had changed you and sent you here. Don't reckon He messed up, do you?"

Redd's words shot through him like a jolt of electricity. "Well, I don't see any way to fix things with the Williamses. But I'd like to think I can fix things with you."

His dad motioned toward the cash register. Mark followed.

Redd rang up the tarps, slowly, one by one. "I'm trying not to be mad about the money anymore. I see you were just trying to help."

Despite all that had happened between them, his dad finally seemed to want to mend the past. Mark leaned on the counter, the tension easing from his body. If only his dad could overlook the pain Mark had caused and love him for the person he was today. "I wasn't trying to make you feel bad. I really did—do—want to help. Will you let me pay the taxes?"

"Nope. But I had some time to think while cowering back in the supply closet during that storm."

Dare he hope? He didn't move a muscle. *Lord, please*...

His dad gazed off toward one of the windows. "I'd heard the storm was heading out your way. Scared me to death."

He'd worried about him? "The kids and I huddled in the bathroom. We were fine."

"If something happened—" he shoved another tarp into a shopping bag "—and I hadn't eased your mind…"

"Eased my mind?"

Redd handed over the bags for Mark to put in the cart. "I didn't want you to carry that guilt you've been hauling around all these years. I'd never forgive myself if you died thinking…thinking I didn't care."

"I ruined so many lives, Dad."

"You didn't ruin anyone's but your own—with all that drinking."

The alcohol had been a symptom. A response to cope with the heartache. "But Matt…" Mark's throat suddenly convulsed, catching him off guard. "I know his death was my fault. I'm so sorry."

Mark couldn't even look at his dad. He stared into the cart, at all those tarps, a temporary fix for holes in roofs, but there wasn't a single thing he could do to fix the gaping wound in his heart.

A warm, roughened hand covered Mark's own. "It wasn't your fault."

Mark stared at his dad's hand. And he could suddenly remember the good times. Dad teaching him to use tools. Teaching him to take things apart and put them back together. Teaching him to build—the satisfaction of creating. All those moments had led to Mark's love of building things—a love that had given him the desire to make something of his life. To quit drinking and go back to school.

Mark searched his dad's eyes, so much like his own. Eyes devoid of condemnation, warm with forgiveness. "If I hadn't talked him into going out in your boat, even though you'd forbidden it, even though I knew he couldn't swim…Matt wouldn't have fallen in or contracted pneumonia. He'd be alive today."

"You were just doing stuff teenage boys do. And you saved him from drowning."

Yeah, too little, too late. "But you blamed me. Mom did, too. Losing Matt killed her. She went to bed and didn't get back up. You couldn't even look at me."

"I was ashamed. I insisted you take him with you that day. Mom asked me to watch Matt while she worked at vacation Bible school, and I was too busy here at the store to bother. So I shooed you both out, told you to take him with you." He breathed in several heavy breaths. "It was my fault your brother died. Took your mother years to forgive me. But with God's help, we healed and moved on."

Stunned, Mark couldn't utter a sound. He searched his dad's eyes, to see if he was just trying to make Mark feel better. But he obviously spoke the truth. "Then why were you so angry when I came back here?"

"The anger was at how your leaving hurt your mother, and the lack of contact worried us sick. Then shame over the condition of the house." He shrugged. "Mostly guilt. I withdrew after Matt died and wasn't there for you. I knew your leaving was my fault, as well."

Mark sighed. So many years. So much guilt and pain. "I'm sorry for leaving. And more, for not coming home sooner. Can you forgive me?"

"Son, you don't need to be the one asking. Can *you* forgive me?"

Lord, thank You for leading me here. And for this moment. "Of course." He reached over and squeezed his dad's hand. "I love you."

Redd swiped at a tear. "Love you, too."

Mark went around the counter and embraced his dad, who hugged him back, then ended with a hearty pat on the back.

"I'm glad to have you home, son. Will you stay longer?"

"I can't. I'm starting to care too much for a certain neighbor of yours."

"I understand. Could you hang around and try to win Donna over?"

He gave his dad a crooked *Are you kidding me?* smile.

"She's a hard woman who won't let go of a

grudge. But I'd say Hannah is worth the groveling." Redd's eyes twinkled, as if he knew facing Donna would test Mark's courage.

"Sticking around for Hannah is definitely worth any wrath I may feel. But I can't put Hannah or her children through that."

"If Hannah cares for you, I hate to see her hurt. But you do what you think is best. I'm hoping you'll come back again to visit."

"How about if I come back for Thanksgiving?"

He nodded, his face breaking into a smile. He clapped Mark on the back. "I'd like that, son."

Hannah tried her best not to let on to the kids how upset she was with her mother. She also didn't want them to know about having to go to day care until she had the chance to sit down with them at home and explain.

But how could she possibly explain that their grandmother was blinded by unforgiveness? That she hadn't yet learned to trust Hannah's judgment and thought she was protecting them?

Hoping they didn't get too muddy, she sent them to play in the grass in front of the courthouse while she sat on the bench to call her friend Bev, the director of the only child-care center in town.

"Hi, Bev. I need your help."

"Fire away."

"Long story short, I need summer child care. If they can start at the center tomorrow, I'd need to drop them off at—"

"We're full, Hannah. I'm so sorry. Our adult-kid ratio is maxed out. But I can add you to the waiting list."

Oh, no. She'd never considered it would be full. "Do you have any idea how long it might be?"

"I can't afford to hire another worker until I get eight more kids on the list. Even with your four, I doubt we'll get that many this summer."

Squeezing back tears, she shut her eyes. "Thanks, Bev. Go ahead and add them to the list. I'll start praying."

"I'll pray, too, sweetie. Hang in there."

What could she do? Miss Ann was too old to watch them full-time. She didn't trust teenagers to handle four children, so that ruled out all the potential babysitters from the youth group. Maybe she could find a college student. Or a stay-at-home mom who'd take in her brood for some extra money.

Money. She had to pay for this. Out of her house fund.

With clenched fists and gritted teeth, she rounded up the kids to go to the hardware store. She needed to let Redd know about the roof and broken windows. Maybe Mark would show up with tarps and temporary window covering.

The thought of seeing him made the frustration and anger dissipate as they entered the store. She tried her best to keep all little hands out of the bins of nuts and bolts and all things shiny and tempting.

Redd came over to meet them. "Hi, there, Hannah. Glad to see you're all okay."

"Thank the Lord, we're all fine. Did Mark fill you in on the house?"

"He did. I'm relieved we didn't have more damage."

"We probably need a tarp for one part of the roof. And I wanted to check with you on getting the glass replaced."

"Don't worry about it. I'll bring home everything we need. Mark's already been by here to buy tarps to distribute around town. I'm sure he has one for you and will take care of it."

She'd been right about Mark. For the second time that day, he'd watched out for her. His consideration warmed her to her toes. "Oh, good. We'll head home now and wait for him."

"He may already be there. But...well...you should know something."

The look on his face and the serious tone of his voice made her heart sink. "What is it?"

He looked over at the kids, who raked their hands through a bin of key rings. He leaned toward her ear. "He plans to leave town tonight."

As if someone had yanked the floor out from under her, she swayed. "Oh. W-why?"

"It's his place to fill you in."

The storm, trouble with her mom, day-care issues…and now Mark was leaving? Would this nightmarish day never end?

Tears brimmed, then ran down her cheeks. When Tony looked up, concerned, she darted between shelves so the kids wouldn't see her.

Redd followed and awkwardly patted her shoulder. "Hon, it'll be okay. Maybe you can talk some sense into him."

She swiped the traitorous drops away, furious at her mother. His leaving now had to be Donna's fault. "I'm sorry. It's been a stressful day."

"I know. Go on home. Get some rest. Don't fret. Mark and I will handle the repairs."

Except Mark wouldn't be there long enough to handle anything.

He was leaving. Tonight.

The children were quiet all the way home, as if they sensed her distress. Of course, they'd witnessed the spectacle she'd made in front of Redd.

When they arrived at the house, Mark was sawing a fallen tree into pieces. And a blue tarp already covered the damaged roof.

Tears welled up once again, but rather than let Mark see them, she pressed at the inner corners of her eyes so tightly it hurt. Better than letting him see her crying over the fact that he was leaving her.

She knew it had to be best that he go. Yet somewhere in the back of her mind, she'd nursed a flicker of hope he would stick it out with Donna. Would find Hannah worth fighting for.

Tony, obviously thrilled to see Mark—his new hero—ran over. "Can I help?"

"No, son. I'm afraid you're too young for power tools—as your mom so nicely told me a while back." He smiled at her, and she knew he was truly leaving. The smile held sadness. Maybe even regret.

"Come on, everyone. We need to go inside and let Mark work." She nodded to acknowledge him but couldn't look him in the eye. He might see how his plan to leave was wounding her. "Thank you for covering the roof. And for getting that tree out of the way."

"Glad to help."

She shepherded the kids inside and tried her best to ignore that Mark was outside. As she swept up broken glass, she decided she wouldn't let him go without at least trying to talk some sense into him.

She put the kids to work cleaning their rooms and marched back outside, determined to change his mind.

As she neared him, she lost some of the steam.

How could she change his mind without telling him how she felt about him?

How could she risk telling him when he and her mother were at odds?

When he saw her, he turned off the saw. "So, are the kids worn-out from their wild day?"

"I hear you're leaving."

He ran his hand over his chin, bristly with a five-o'clock shadow, and squinted at the late-afternoon sun, so out of place after the storm. He looked...drained. Her heart thumped with worry.

He finally looked straight at her. "Yes. Tonight."

"Why?" she bit out, but her voice betrayed her as it cracked.

"I think you know why."

Yes, she knew. Because earlier, after the storm, she'd hugged him, had laid her face near his heart and wished for things she couldn't have. She'd sensed he wished for the same. "My mother."

"I don't want to cause conflict in your family. I've done enough of that."

He was really going to leave. Her brain clicked at high speed as she tried to find reasons for him to stay. Acceptable reasons, not reasons like her missing him or relying on him when she hadn't dared rely on someone in years. "But what about making things right with your dad?"

A smile drained the tension from his face. "We talked, like you suggested. Thanks to you, and

God's work on both our hearts, Dad's forgiven me. He also asked *my* forgiveness."

"That's wonderful. God can bring about good from any situation." Her own smile tried to wobble. She truly was happy for him. But now he was free to leave. Before he'd given God a chance to work on healing his relationship with her mother.

Should she ask him to stay? "Do you think you'll ever consider relocating? Returning...you know...home?"

Staring off into the pasture, he ran a hand through his dusty hair. "I've had a few large corporations approach me about selling—one recently." He looked into her eyes. "But I turned them down. Can't imagine turning over control of something I started from the ground up."

So his career was important enough to keep him in Seattle. "Well, I need to let you work." She had to pull herself away. While she could.

"I'll let you know when I'm done out here."

She nodded and headed back toward the house.

No, she couldn't ask him to stay. Besides, Mark's leaving proved she couldn't depend on anyone to take care of her. Anyone but God. And herself.

Ax in hand, Mark attacked the logs, releasing pent up tension, sending wood chips flying.

He split the wood as if hacking at his own feelings. Feelings for a woman he had no right to care about.

Swing. Chop.

Sure she's beautiful, but she's Sydney's sister.

Sure she's smart and generous and kind, but I'm the jerk who destroyed her family and made her lose her home.

Sure she's an amazing mother, but her mother hates me.

By the time he had a neatly stacked pile of wood beside the garage, he'd worn out his arms and back. But he still hadn't gotten Hannah out of his heart.

He put away the ax and wiped his brow with the shoulder of his T-shirt. He looked around the property at what he'd managed to complete in a couple of weeks. Much more needed to be done. Work he'd have to leave for his dad.

The unfinished rocking chairs on the porch bugged him most. They still needed primer and fresh coats of white paint to bring them back to how he remembered from his childhood. Now they looked sad, weathered, beaten.

The sun had lowered on the horizon, its pinks and purples offering a spectacular display of God's creation. If only he and Hannah could sit on the porch and watch it together...

No. He needed to go by Ann's for his things and head to Atlanta.

He dusted off his hands and climbed the porch.

At his knock, Becca answered, then laughed. "Mr. Mark, you have wood stuff all over you."

"I'm a mess, aren't I?" He knelt down in front of her. "I wanted to tell you all goodbye."

"Are you going to Miss Ann's?"

"No, I'm leaving to go back to my own house across the country."

Hannah and the other children walked up behind Becca.

"But we like having you here." Becca turned to her siblings. "He's going away."

"I'll be back to visit on Thanksgiving."

He glanced at the twins' sad faces.

Emily's lip quivered. "Mr. Mark, we have so much fun with you."

"Then we'll make big holiday plans with lots of fun, okay?"

"Okay," Eric and Emily said in unison.

He looked at Tony, and the stoic expression on the boy's face socked him in the gut. "Hey, big guy. Maybe when I come back, you can help me paint the railing here on the porch. Deal?"

Without the slightest show of emotion, Tony turned and walked away.

With no idea what to do or say, Mark rose and

looked at Hannah. The stricken look on her face ripped his insides to shreds.

"Kids, can I talk to your mom alone for a minute, please?"

They hugged him, and he thought his heart might break at the thought of leaving them. At the thought he wouldn't see them for five months. They'd probably grow an inch. Would be in school. Might need homework help.

Hannah peeled them off of him and sent them inside. They'd gotten so attached to him so quickly.

Who was he kidding? He'd gotten even more attached to them. "I'll tell Dad the kids are a little sad right now and see if he'll spend some extra time with them."

"Okay. Thanks for everything. For the house…" Her hands fluttered as she vaguely pointed to the property. Then she shrugged. "For the babysitting." Her eyelids fluttered.

Was she blinking at tears?

Oh, man. He had to get out of there. Reaching to push her hair back from her face, he realized his hands were dirty. He was covered in sawdust. So he pulled away and shoved his hands in his pockets. "Gotta go. See you at Thanksgiving."

He forced himself to turn and walk away. Forced himself into the car. Forced himself not to watch in the rearview mirror as she stood there waving while he drove down the driveway.

That peaceful arch of trees closed in behind him, shutting him off from those who had somehow, miraculously, become important to him.

Leaving was for the best. For Hannah.

But was it best for him?

No matter. He had a company to run in Seattle. Though he'd had multimillion-dollar offers to buy him out, he couldn't imagine selling. What could he possibly do to follow up on that kind of success?

He tried calling Ann but didn't get an answer. He'd missed dinner, so he stopped at the café to pick up a sandwich and see if Ann might be there. She wasn't. And neither was the owner, Faith. A young man he hadn't seen before waited on him.

As the guy bagged the ham sandwich and poured him a cup of coffee to go, Mark heard his name somewhere around the corner, behind the espresso machine. A woman was talking about him. Loud enough for him—and probably everyone else in the shop—to hear.

"Well, he was nice enough to bring a tarp by my house today," said a quiet voice he didn't recognize.

"I don't think he's changed a bit," said the loud one. "I still say he's taking advantage of Ann."

"Maybe."

The café employee punched Mark's items into

the cash register, glancing between Mark and the
women around the corner, his face red.

"I think y'all need to give him a chance to prove
he's changed," said the kind one.

"And wait until he's hurt Ann…and maybe even
Hannah?"

"Hannah?"

The young man told Mark the order total in a
loud voice, trying to cover for his gossiping customers.

Apparently, he knew who Mark was.

"Haven't you heard he's been hanging out at her
house, watching her kids?"

"No way!" said a third person. This voice was
familiar, but he couldn't place it.

"Well, that's plain strange," said the quiet one.
"Maybe you're right. Maybe he's up to something.
Hannah's pretty. And I bet there was a life-insur-
ance policy."

Mark couldn't stomach another word. He threw
a twenty on the counter, thanked the boy and
snatched the bag out of his hand before he'd finished stuffing napkins inside.

Mark couldn't get out of there fast enough.
Couldn't get out of Corinthia fast enough.

As he started the car and peeled away from the
curb, an ache seared his chest, squeezing until
he thought it might bruise his heart. He would
never belong in this town. No matter what his dad

thought of him. No matter what Hannah and her kids thought of him.

If he couldn't get a flight out of Atlanta tonight, he'd climb back in the rental car and start driving. Because he couldn't get out of Georgia fast enough.

Chapter Ten

Hannah pushed past the hurt and forced her mind off Mark's leaving. She needed to focus on the challenge at hand. She refused to call her mother and tell her she'd won. But she still needed child care.

She first called Gabe for recommendations on college students who were home for the summer. After trying all three girls, and finding they already had jobs, she still didn't have a babysitter for the next day. It looked as if she would have to call her mother after all.

But not yet. She couldn't deal with Donna gloating, not when she felt so sad and defeated.

After a late, and very quiet, dinner of peanut-butter-and-jelly sandwiches—which reminded the kids of Mark—they trudged to their rooms, moping.

When she went to check on them, Emily and

Eric sat together on the bed looking at an *I Spy* book. No yelling. No competing to see who found an item first.

Curled up in her favorite chair, Becca read her newest library book.

Tony lay curled up on his bed, and it broke Hannah's heart. He'd opened his wounded heart to Mark, only to have him leave.

"Hey, sweetie. You okay?" She rubbed his back.

"Yeah."

The way he was curved, she could feel each vertebra, could count them. "Are you sad that Mark's leaving?"

He shrugged.

"I'll miss him, too."

He sniffed. "You will?"

How could she not? "Yes. He's a kind man. Fun to have around. And very helpful."

"So, do you like him?"

"Yes. He's nice."

"I mean *like him* like him."

What would her son know about that type of liking someone? "As a boyfriend? No. We're just friends."

"Well, if he's your friend, why is he leaving?"

Because sometimes life wasn't fair. "This isn't his home. He lives in Washington State."

"Well, shouldn't he live where his dad and his friends live?"

Good point. She patted his back. "That's where his job is. People live where they work."

He rolled to his back and looked at her with those thoughtful, inquisitive green eyes. "Is Washington State farther away than Heaven?"

Pain snatched the very air from her lungs and left her aching, wanting to lie down in a little ball and join her son. "No, baby. It's a long way, but it's here in the United States. You can fly there on an airplane."

And Mark was about to do just that.

What if she asked him to stay? She nearly had earlier. Would it have made a difference?

Tony's eyes widened. "Can we fly there sometime?"

"Someday. We sure will."

What if she went to him and admitted her feelings? Would he consider selling his company?

Her heart thudded up into her throat. He could say no.

But he could say yes.

She hurried to the phone and dialed Redd. "I need a big favor. Could you please hurry home and watch the children for me?"

"Everything okay?"

"I need to go catch your son before he leaves."

"I'm locking up and walking out the door as we speak."

Bless his heart. Not only was she falling in love with Mark, she loved his father, as well.

She hurried to get the children ready for bed. And hoped she got to Ann's house in time.

Mark showered and changed. He didn't have much to pack. Had been washing and wearing the same four changes of clothes the whole time. He threw the clothes back in the bag, loaded the car and spent a few minutes with Ann.

"Thank the good Lord you and your daddy made up. I expect to see you soon."

"I promise." He hugged her, breathing in her perfume. "You taking me in means more to me than I can ever repay."

"Oh, it was no bother at all. I loved your company."

"You're a kind, generous woman. I hope I can return the favor for somebody else someday."

She kissed his cheek, blinked at tears. "Go on, now, before you make me start crying. Besides, you don't need to be driving so late."

His insides warmed that someone cared about his safety, like a mom would. He waved and headed to the car.

As he shifted into Reverse, a vehicle pulled in behind—the green minivan.

Hannah. Hannah had come.

He turned off the car and climbed out, his heart

pumping in his chest. The sun had set, and the streetlight illuminated the end of the driveway. He thought she might be smiling, but the shadows made it impossible to tell. She approached so slowly, he held his breath. "Everything okay?"

"It is now that I caught you in time." She stopped right in front of him, so close he could smell her flowery, sweet scent.

This time, instead of holding back, he brushed his fingers through the silky strands of hair at the side of her face. "Did you need something?"

She nuzzled his hand, sending electrons zipping through the circuits of his body. "Yes. I need you."

Blood rushed to his head. *She needs me?* "Something wrong at the house?"

"Yes, definitely." She smiled up at him.

And he knew she could ask for anything…everything…and he would try to get it for her. "I can stop by there now. My flight doesn't leave until 5:00 a.m."

"I don't think you quite understand."

"I must be missing something here."

"Please don't go back to Seattle. Stay, finish your vacation. Take more time to consider relocating. Back here. With me."

But he *had* to go now. If she kept standing that close, asking him to stay, he wouldn't be able to leave.

Ever.

"I'm leaving to make life easier for you. Let me be the hero for once." He smiled, but it went crooked. He'd heard those ladies talking earlier. He was no hero in Corinthia. No matter how hard he tried, he'd never be accepted in this town.

"Mark, I want you to stay." She looked into his eyes, hers pleading. "My children are moping and miss you already."

He tilted up her chin. "And what about their mom? Would she miss me, as well?"

"Yes, terribly."

She was scared to admit it. But he could see the need in her eyes. The confusion, too. Which he understood perfectly.

He ran his thumb along her velvety cheek. "I think neither of us is ready to closely examine our feelings."

"We can take our time. And meanwhile, maybe you can connect with those potential corporate buyers, consider the possibilities?"

When she was this close, he thought anything was possible. "Okay, I'll stay for now, finish my vacation. But I'll only consider relocating if I can win over Donna."

A smile lit her eyes, making them sparkle in the streetlight. "Thank you. We at least have a chance to see what happens."

"I know what I want to happen right this minute." His eyes dropped to her lips. Slowly, he low ered his head, giving her time to move away. Time to change her mind about getting involved with the totally wrong man. With a man her mother loathed.

She didn't budge. And then she touched him, her hand as light as a butterfly on his chest. "Mark," she said on a whisper, so close that his name brushed across his own lips.

It was the only invitation he needed. He touched his lips to hers, trying to take it slow and give her time to back out. But as soon as she wrapped her arms around his neck, he was lost.

Lost in the moment. In the taste of her. In the need to be closer. His heart thundered as he deepened the kiss. Longing for…for…

For more than two weeks. Longing for love. Commitment. A lifetime…

She pulled away, gasping for air the same as he did.

She touched her lips. "That's the first—" Tears welled up in her eyes.

Whoa. He needed to consider her feelings and be tender. "The first time you've kissed a man since your husband?"

She nodded. He thought she might cry, so he hugged her close. Ran his hands through her hair. "It's okay. He would want you to be happy."

"I know," she whispered against his chest. "And

I'm good. Really. The tears are because I'm re-lieved to move on."

But he wasn't relieved at all. He'd never expe-rienced a kiss like that. Never experienced what they'd shared. And it shook him to the core.

He loved Hannah Hughes.

How would he ever leave Corinthia now?

Hannah's toes were still curled. Her lips still tingled. Even ten hours after what she had begun to think of as *The Kiss*.

She closed her eyes and swayed on her feet.

She'd been as excited to see Mark as the kids had been when they heard he was staying longer.

"What's wrong, Mommy?" Emily asked.

Laughter wanted to bubble up and out. "Oh, nothing, sweetie." She tossed the dish towel onto the counter. "Come on, now, finish your breakfast before Mark gets here."

"Yeah!" Tony yelled as he raced to put his cereal bowl in the dishwasher. "I hope we prime the rocking chairs today."

"Looks like beautiful weather ahead, so maybe you can." The happy, excited faces of her children made everything brighter. She looked forward to the day.

And maybe that kiss had just a little to do with her high spirits. That and the fact Mark seemed to care about her. *Her.* He'd hung with her through adversity. Had been there when she needed him.

And he'd agreed to stay longer.

A few minutes later, a horn honked outside. The kids raced to meet Mark's car as Hannah waited on the porch, hesitant to face him. Would he see the love on her face in the light of day? See her need for him?

He hugged each child, but the whole time, he stared toward her, as if he only had eyes for her.

Yes, he sees me. *Not my sister. Not my mother. Not our past.*

She smiled at him, no longer embarrassed. "You're early."

He walked up the steps and stopped a couple of feet away, as if aware the kids were watching every move. "Wouldn't miss a minute with this bunch."

"Thank you. It's nice to know I have someone to depend on."

"No matter what happens or where I live, you can always depend on me, Hannah."

The way he said her name—husky, sincere— and the intensity of his gaze…

His golden eyes rooted her to the spot. Could she really depend on him? Experience told her not to depend on others. They could let her down, or get sick, even die. Or choose other priorities over her.

She reached inside the door and grabbed her

purse. "I should go. I've got to stop by the coffee shop to place an order for a breakfast meeting. Even so, I'll be early at the bank this morning." The joy she'd felt all morning actually did bubble out into a laugh this time. "The tellers won't know what to do."

As she walked by him, he reached out and grasped her hand. A discreet, passing touch. "Have a great day."

The touch and warmth of his tone sent her heart rate into the stratosphere. "Thanks, Mark. For everything."

As she waited in the short line at Faith's coffee shop, she spotted a table of ladies, including—surprisingly—her mom, who waved her over. She pointed to her watch. "Can't. I need to get to work."

But Faith's employees served the line quickly, so she made a stop by the table. "Good morning, ladies."

With a big grin on her face, Olivia leaned toward Hannah. "Did you hear Mark Ryker was going to leave town, had loaded the car, then suddenly changed his mind?"

Ann gave Hannah a distressed look. "Oh, now, Olivia, we don't need to be talking about his business."

"No one told me about this," Donna said. "I've

been here a half hour. Why didn't someone mention it?"

Hannah's stomach clenched into a tight, painful knot. "Got to go to work. Just wanted to stop by and say hello."

"You know something?" Donna asked as she grabbed Hannah's arm to stop her.

Ann's neighbor Jeannie waved her hand, as if excited to take her turn to enlighten everyone. "I saw him load his luggage into the car around nine last night. I assumed he'd left."

"I heard a certain someone stopped him," Olivia said with a thrilled smile, as if she couldn't be happier about it. She tried not to look at Hannah, but her eyes darted that direction anyway.

Had someone witnessed their kiss? The thought of someone invading their private moment, a moment so special, made her queasy.

"He's bad news," her mom said. "I sure hope no one I know made the mistake of getting involved with him."

"He's not bad news," Hannah snapped. "You're judging him by his behavior fifteen years ago. He's grown up. Has been through a lot. And is a Christian man with a good heart." She sucked in air after her tirade, and it turned into a big gasp.

But it wasn't as big as the gasp that came out of her mother. "Oh, Hannah. No. You didn't fall for him." Her eyes probed Hannah's, searching for denial.

Everyone at the table went silent. Still. Waiting. Even as Hannah knew all her mother would see was confirmation.

Ann clutched Hannah's hand. Hannah knew the tight grip meant she was praying.

Hannah raised her chin and looked her mother in the eye. "Yes. I have feelings for him. He's helping me as we speak. Changed his plans to stay longer. He'll watch the children for me until I can arrange day care."

Donna stood, bumping her chair backward across the floor, causing it to tip over. The slap of the wood on the tile floor echoed through the now-quiet café. "If you start seeing *that Ryker man,*" she spat with venom, "I won't have any contact with you or the kids. None. I won't condone a relationship that I know will be devastating for you and my grandbabies."

If she didn't let go of this ridiculous grudge, Mark would leave. "Mom, please. Give him a chance to prove himself."

Wringing her hands in front of her chest, she blinked at tears. "You're out of my life until you send him packing."

Ann's grip tightened, mashing Hannah's fingers until they hurt. Hannah squeezed back even tighter. "If your grudge is stronger than your love for your grandchildren, then maybe they're better off."

The color drained from Donna's red face.

Hannah couldn't bear to look at the women around the table. Tears burned her eyes as she let go of Ann and struggled to make it out of the café before breaking down.

But as she walked outside into the fresh morning air and breathed in deeply, peace only God could provide washed over her. *This is the right thing to do.*

She walked to the bank, having no idea how it would work out. Only that with God's help, it *would* work out.

As long as Mark could wait for God's timing. As long as he cared enough to try.

Chapter Eleven

On Saturday morning, Mark rang the doorbell of Hannah's home—yes, he'd come to think of it as her home now. Though Redd had invited him to stay in the garage apartment, he'd decided to continue staying with Ann, who had more room.

He stuck his head inside and hollered, "I need some workers to help paint the porch railing!"

The tramping of little feet echoed upstairs, as well as from the kitchen area. The ruckus got louder as they all reached the front door at the same time.

"I'll help!" Tony shouted over his siblings, who were also volunteering with hands raised.

Hannah arrived a few seconds later in rolled-up denim overalls with her hair in a ponytail on top of her head. Barefoot. "I'm ready to work, too."

"You look…amazing. Beautiful."

She glanced down at her worn work clothes. "In these old things?"

All he could see was the woman he'd grown to care about. Sweet. Kind. And wanting to spend time with him. "In anything," he rasped. Before he made a fool of himself, he turned and led them outside.

The refurbished chairs now sat proudly on the front porch, a reminder of better times. And now a promise…maybe…of happy times to come. But the porch rails were chipped and peeling.

"Why don't you and the kids trim the shrubbery while I sand the railing?"

"I'll help you," Tony said. Then he leaned closer and whispered, "It's man's work."

"Sure is. I'd appreciate your help."

They worked without a break until lunchtime. Then after a quick meal of egg-salad sandwiches, they started the priming and painting. Mark put down drop cloths. He'd have to do some cleaning up from letting the little ones help. But seeing their smiles and sense of accomplishment would be worth every drip and smear of paint.

After an hour or so, Hannah got worried about the kids getting sunburned, even with sunscreen. So she took them inside to rest and read. Then she rejoined him outside.

He put down his paintbrush and asked her to sit with him on the top step. His heart thrilled when she sat close, her leg touching his, at ease. Resting his arm around her waist felt as natural as breathing.

She looked up at him with bright green eyes—the green of emeralds, of early summer leaves, of—

"I've had fun today," she said, interrupting his fanciful thoughts. "We still need to repaint the siding, but it's nice to see the house sparkling once again."

"My mom and dad used to sit out here on evenings my dad left the store early. And on Sunday evenings. I'd hear them talking in low tones, and laughing. Those sounds made me happy. Made me feel secure."

She gave him a wistful smile. "I'm glad you have those good memories. My mom and dad laughed a lot early on, too."

He noticed she didn't go into the hard times. The later times, after he came into their lives. "I'm sorry for the troubles I caused."

"It wasn't all your fault. Dad always had a hard time dealing with Mom's negativity and controlling nature. I'm pretty sure they already had financial difficulties, as well."

Trying to take comfort from her words, he nodded. "Still, I'd like to hear that you forgive me, if you think you can."

She put her hands on each side of his face. They

were warm, and smelled like summer. "I forgive you. You're a good man, and I'm glad God led you home. If He hadn't, I might still be holding on to anger and resentment." She gave him a quick, soft kiss. "I'm grateful He brought us together even if it's just for a short time. Though I'm hopeful for longer."

He put his hands over hers, encasing his face, and leaned in for another, more satisfying kiss. When he pulled away, he told himself not to get used to this closeness. Not to depend on any kind of relationship until he'd won over Donna. He touched his forehead to hers. "Thank you, Hannah."

"As much as I'd rather sit here, we need to finish the last section of the porch." She popped up to her feet and grabbed his paintbrush. Then she brushed a streak of paint down his forearm. "Oops."

"Why, you..." He dashed after her across the porch as she squealed in laughter. When she dodged his grasp and darted down the steps, he grabbed another brush. He caught up to her in the yard and dabbed the brush on her nose.

She gasped in shock, then quickly followed it with a burst of laughter. He spun to the side. Felt the brush slap him on the back as he tried to arch, but couldn't manage to get away.

Squeals—kids' squeals—sounded on the porch.

He stopped long enough to look up. Into four laughing faces.

"We're not a very good example to your children right now," he called to Hannah as he made another lunge in her direction.

"Oh, I beg to differ." She grabbed at a stitch in her side, then doubled over with a big belly laugh.

He caught up to her easily, and once she stood, he wrapped his arms around her waist. "So you consider this art lessons?"

When she smiled up at him, the dollop of white paint on her nose rather cute, he thought he'd never seen anyone so perfect in his life. "No. They're getting to see two people in—" Her eyes flared open. "Having fun together."

Had she been about to say two people in love?

"Are you going to kiss?" Becca called in a very rational tone of voice, as if observing a science experiment.

Risking kisses with Hannah alone was one thing. But not in front of her children. They might get their hopes up. "No, we're just playing."

She stepped away from him. "We were being silly. And now look at the mess we made." She wiped a smear off his cheek, and gave him a sad smile. They both wanted something they couldn't have.

Yet

Everything would be perfect if only he could convince Donna he meant Hannah no harm.

He would try to talk to her on Sunday.

Hannah couldn't wait to see Mark at the worship service Sunday morning. They'd only been apart twelve hours, yet she longed to be near him.

She knew she shouldn't allow herself to look forward to something so much. So many issues stood between them—her mother, her sister, his business.

Not exactly an auspicious beginning for a relationship.

"Will we get to see Nana today?" Tony asked as they walked in the church sanctuary, reminding her she needed to settle down and quit being so distracted. He stood on his toes, looking toward their regular pew, searching for his grandmother.

She rubbed his back and did her own search. No Donna in sight. "I hope so." But she knew better. Her mother was always early. If she wasn't there now, she wouldn't be coming.

Mom, please. Please don't do this to the children.

She searched the sanctuary for her mother. No sign of her anywhere. As Hannah and the kids started down the aisle, Redd stood up and motioned for them to come down front to where he sat.

With Mark.

She couldn't help smiling at seeing the two of them together, totally relaxed. But then she realized, too late, her smile had indicated to the kids that they should respond to his summons. The four of them raced ahead and zipped into the pew between the two men.

What could she do but follow? When she arrived, Mark stepped out into the aisle to let her enter.

"Good morning," he said as she slipped in and took the only seat available. Between him and the kids.

"Good morning." What was she doing? Sitting with the Rykers was practically advertising a relationship with Mark. Her mother was sure to hear about it. She leaned toward his ear. "I'm not sure this is a good idea."

"I tried to stop my dad, but he said Donna isn't here today, so you might need help with the kids."

His breath tickled her ear, sending goose bumps down her bare arms.

"Cold?" He took off his jacket and settled it over her shoulders.

The man had noticed her chill. He was that attentive.

Between the warmth of the jacket that smelled like him—fresh and clean—and the warmth of the attention, she wasn't feeling inclined to move away. For the first time in years, she felt secure. Protected.

And in all honesty, she could use some help. Emily and Eric usually had a difficult time sitting through a whole service without getting antsy. She relished having two extra adults to watch them.

She tried to rationalize the sense of joy. She had every right to make decisions that were best for her family. That would make them happy. But she hated the thought of her mother at home, refusing to associate with them…refusing to attend the worship service—all because Hannah had stuck up for Mark.

It sucked the joy out of the moment.

Her breathing quickened. Heat washed up her neck and face as she imagined an opportunity to tell her mother how wrong she was. If the woman had a legitimate beef with Mark, that would be one thing. But he'd apologized. He'd changed his life.

Donna was being stubborn and unforgiving. Hannah couldn't let that influence her choices in relationships.

In a moment of rebellion, she scooted a little closer to Mark.

Mark glanced down at Hannah, who'd scooted right up next to him earlier in the service. He wanted nothing more than to have her by his side.

But not yet. Not when he hadn't earned her mother's respect. He couldn't put Hannah and her children in the middle.

The sooner he made amends, the better.

"Why don't we all go out to eat?" Redd said as they filed out of the church. "I'm buying."

Hannah glanced at Mark. "Well, the kids and I don't have plans."

Going out to eat as a virtual family might not be a good idea.

A little warm hand slipped into his. When he looked down, he found Becca staring up at him.

She pushed up her pink glasses with one finger and squinted to hold them there. "Are you coming, too?"

A quick glance at Hannah made his decision. *Hope.* He saw hope in her eyes. And fear. And maybe some longing?

"I wouldn't miss it," he told Becca as he gave her hand a gentle squeeze.

They all walked across the street to Frank's Pizza Place. Frank, who'd opened the business when Mark was a child, waved and smiled. He never said much, but he made the best pizza in three counties.

Once they'd ordered, Redd leaned back in his seat. "So, Hannah, how's the fundraising going for the mission trip?"

She gave a little snort and grinned at his dad. "Do you have to ask?"

Mark looked between his dad and Hannah. "What's up with the trip?"

"Hannah called a while back to ask if the store could sponsor a child for the mission trip. I agreed to sponsor one. Then when I took your money out of my account, I passed it on to Hannah for the youth. Now I can sponsor...well, several kids."

Mark had been learning about giving. Learning to acknowledge that all he'd worked for and earned was a gift from God. Seeing the joy on his dad's face at the possibility of helping others was humbling. "Hannah, I'd like to sponsor some of the kids, too."

Redd clapped him on the back and smiled. "Son, you just did."

Mark was happy they could laugh about what had been a difficult situation before. A smile crept up on him.

Hannah took hold of Mark's and Redd's hands. "The generosity of both of you has financed the whole trip. We've also set aside part of the money to help with scholarships next year. Gabe is hopeful it'll become an annual, church-wide event, growing each year."

She plastered a proud look on her face. "We won't turn away another donation, though. You could always contribute to the ski-trip scholarships. And retreats. And local mission projects. Maybe a matching program. You'll match whatever the youth make on their fundraising projects."

Mark nodded. "I like it. They'll have to do their share of the work."

"Of course. They're hard workers when it comes to their projects."

"You've sold me. I'll contact Gabe when I get back to Seattle."

The comment was like a splash of cold water in his face. And, apparently, on Hannah, too. The grip of her slender hand slackened, and she pulled it away.

"Seattle is in Washington state," Tony told Redd. "It's clear across the country. Like a thousand miles away."

Redd whistled. "That far, huh?"

"Yeah. But not as far away as Heaven."

Mark's eyes shot to Hannah's. The weight of what he needed to do sank in.

There was a lot more at stake here than just his and Hannah's feelings for each other. Hannah was a package deal.

A relationship with her was also a relationship with four children who'd lost their father.

He would go talk to Donna as soon as they finished lunch. This time, success was critical.

* * *

Donna stared at Mark through a small opening in the door.

"You don't have any business here," she said as she slammed the door shut—on the foot he'd inserted.

"Please. I'm worried about Tony and need to talk with you."

Fear glittered in her angry eyes. "What's wrong?"

"Can I come in? I won't keep you more than ten minutes."

She threw the door open and jerked her head toward a small kitchen at the back of the duplex.

Everything was tidy, spotless. Perfectly matched picture frames, filled with photos of Hannah's kids from birth to the present, lined the short hallway. When they reached the kitchen, he sat at a small wooden table he suspected was clean enough to eat off.

"Talk," she said once she'd sat stiffly across from him.

"I think Tony is getting attached to me."

She shook her head. "Well, duh. He misses his dad."

"And his grandmother."

Eyes squinted, she leaned forward and shook her index finger at him. "Don't you be judging me. I've been there for those kids every minute since Anthony died. But I won't stand by and let Hannah make a huge mistake."

"Is making a statement more important than their feelings? They need you. Hannah needs you."

"You think going off and earning a bundle of money qualifies you to come home and act like you know everything? Well, you don't know a thing."

He ran a hand over his jaw, covering his mouth long enough to keep from saying something he'd regret. "I'm sorry. I don't mean to sound critical. I came here to try one more time to apologize." He rested his arms on the table, trying to read her, trying to understand why she would be so rigid, so hateful. "I know you have every reason to dislike me, but I hope you'll give me a chance to prove I won't hurt your family."

Lines bracketing her eyes and mouth gave her a hard edge. "Do you think avoiding them is easy for me? It's the hardest thing I've ever done. They're my life. My *whole life,* since Sydney's been in rehab." Her grip tightened, bunching up the place mat until her hands shook.

"They miss you. Especially Tony."

"This problem is easily fixed. Leave town."

Her demand hung between them—the sensible solution.

But falling in love wasn't simple.

He took a deep breath and said a quick prayer for fortification. "I care for Hannah, Mrs. Williams. And for the children."

"So? You'll be leaving soon to go back to Seattle and your high-and-mighty job."

"I've made amends with my dad. He's forgiven me. I hope you will, too, so I can feel good about pursuing a relationship with Hannah."

"Do you think I care how you *feel?*" she asked in a voice both soft and menacing. "Did you care how I felt when my Sydney pickled her brain with alcohol? When my husband moved out? When we lost the house because we had to pay for another round of rehab?"

"Please forgive me."

She jerked to her feet, went across the kitchen and yanked the cabinet open. Then she pulled out coffee filters and a tub of Folgers. "I want you to leave."

Somehow, he had to make her understand. "I was devastated by my brother's death. My mother couldn't function. My dad wouldn't even look at me."

She turned her back to him, her hands braced against the counter. "Leave. I don't want to hear your excuses."

"It was all my fault."

She didn't budge. She was a fortress against compassion, waiting for him to go.

"I'm falling in love with her. And I think she cares about me. I hope you'll change your mind... for your daughter's sake."

"I have two daughters. One in her final weeks of rehab. The other in the middle of making the biggest mistake of her life. Anything I do right now is for their sakes."

He forced his legs to carry him outside and away from Donna's house. She'd deliberately brought up Sydney to reinforce the wall between them, a wall that would fuel her grudge.

He would not get Donna Williams's forgiveness.

Chapter Twelve

Hannah had been antsy all evening. Mark had gone to see her mother that afternoon. Now the sun had gone down, and she still hadn't heard from him.

She had the kids bathed and ready for bed and took them out to sit on the porch. Becca and Tony shared one rocker. She held the twins in her lap in the other. But she couldn't stay still. She got up, set them in the chair and paced. Had he and Donna argued? Was he upset and avoiding coming to see her? Had he left town?

The possibilities darting through her mind made her heart race, her breathing shallow. She shouldn't think the worst, though. She knew Mark. He'd babysat her kids. Had protected them. He cared about her. She could trust him. He was probably just spending the day with Ann.

About the time she'd given up on Mark coming

at all, she heard tires crunching gravel along the driveway and then spotted his car—moving way slower than usual. Not a good sign.

She hurried the little ones inside, promising a treat. She would let them watch a movie they'd been dying to see. A reward for behaving so well at church that day.

Once she got the movie set up, she hurried back outside. Mark trudged up to the porch, confirming the worst. She dropped into one rocking chair and pointed to the other. "How bad was it?"

He sat down, closed his eyes. "Pretty bad." The chair rocked back and forth, the wooden joints squeaking with each forward and back motion. Then he tilted his head to look her direction.

"I'm sorry," she said.

"Don't be. She has a right to her anger. My actions cost her everything."

"And now her actions are costing you. So you're even."

He smiled at her in the waning light, his teeth a flash of white. But it quickly faded. She couldn't bear to see him so dejected, so beaten down.

I hurt when he hurts. The realization frightened her. She'd grown to love this man.

Of all the men to fall in love with...

Lord, can I do this? Is this what You want for me? Even against my mother's wishes?

But surely, more than anything, God wanted them to forgive and try to make peace.

Hannah knelt in front of Mark, laying her arms across his knees. "I love you," she whispered. Tears suddenly burned her eyes. Love, fear, compassion all warred inside her.

She refused to let hatred and unforgiveness win. She stared into his eyes, lit only by the light spilling out of the house. "I don't know how this will work out. And I'm scared. But I do know I want you in my life. And in my children's lives."

He stood, tugging her to him. With his strong arms wrapped around her, she felt as if she could take on any challenge.

He nuzzled his cheek to hers. "Hannah, I—"

Oh, please say it. Say you love me, too.

"I can't drive a wedge between your family and your mom. I can't be that person again—the bad boy everyone loathes. I need acceptance. Respect." He stepped away from her, and then he rubbed his hands up and down her arms, as if he knew how his words had chilled her to the bone. "I need to respect myself."

"But I think you care for me, too." So brazen. She couldn't believe she'd said it, but she was going for broke here. "All my life, I've been in Sydney's shadow. But you noticed me. You've made me feel special, wanted. Loved." The last barely came out in a whisper.

He lifted her chin and stared into her eyes, his expression serious, sad. He looked like a man torn. "I do see you. Only you. And I want all this, truly I do."

"Then give us a chance. We'll figure it out. I love my sister and my mother, but I don't want to miss out on this chance at happiness for us, and for my children."

"I want that, too. But not when our relationship is causing strife in your family."

The agony on his face tore at her heart. She reached up and touched his cheek, roughened by the stubble of his beard. "You're trying to be honorable. And I respect that." She exhaled, letting go of the frustration. "We'll just have to be patient."

"Okay." He kissed her palm, the touch of his lips shooting flames along her arm. His lips moved to the inside of her wrist, where he placed the softest of kisses, which left her weak and sighing.

The next thing she knew, he'd enveloped her in his arms and was kissing her as if his life depended on it.

She poured everything into that kiss—every hurt, every longing, every hope—as if she feared it might be their last.

He responded in kind, each press of his lips a silent declaration of his hope for a future together.

He might not be able to tell her he loved her. But she knew he did. In his own honorable way.

The thought gave her hope. He cared enough to stick around, to help with her kids. As long as Mark didn't shut her out, they had a fighting chance.

Mark stood in front of the mirror at Ann's house buttoning his cuffs, smiling. He had a date that night. A real date—no minors as chaperones.

He'd spent the past few days babysitting Hannah's children and spending time with them as a family—Hannah and Redd included. On his trips to town, folks in the community gradually acted more friendly. Maybe Ann's influence. Or his dad's. Either way, they appeared to accept him and accept that he was a part of Hannah's life. He had hope the tide was turning.

He, Hannah and the kids had even run into Donna at the coffee shop one evening getting smoothies for the kids. Though she hadn't acknowledged him or Hannah, she'd at least greeted her grandkids with a hug.

He flipped up his collar and reached for his tie. *Maybe with more time...*

But time was running out. He only had another week in town, so it looked as if he wouldn't be making any big breakthroughs on this trip. Unwilling to call it quits, though, he left his assistant a message asking her to set up meetings with the potential buyers. Maybe if Donna knew he was committed to moving back to Corinthia, he could try to remove that wall between Donna and him one stone at a time.

He tied his tie and adjusted it with a stupid grin on his face. Redd would be babysitting so he and Hannah could go out to dinner. Mark had planned a big surprise for the Valentine's Day she'd wished for. He'd asked at the drugstore, and they'd dug up some cards in the storeroom. He'd ordered flowers and had them delivered to the restaurant. And he'd already enlisted the kids to help him hide some surprises around their house for a treasure hunt.

A fun gift would be waiting at the end of the evening. Becca had assured him she was trustworthy enough to hide it and keep the secret.

Everything was planned and in place. All he had to do was show up.

He threw his suit coat over his arm. As he headed out the door, he called Hannah from his cell phone. "I'm on my way."

A late-model Ford sedan drove up and parked on the street out front. A woman climbed out.

He sucked in a deep breath. "Hannah, your mom just drove up." This could be the moment he'd been praying for.

"Oh, Mark, go. Talk to her. I'll meet you at the restaurant." He could hear the smile in her voice.

"No, I'll call and ask them to move our reservation."

"I don't want to throw off our whole evening. Just meet me there."

Donna strode up the sidewalk.

"Okay. See you there."

He smiled as Donna stepped up onto the porch.

But her face didn't indicate the answer to prayer he'd been hoping for. With scowl firmly in place, the woman's expression was as cold as he'd ever seen it. But he also registered something else in the hazel depths of her eyes. Fear.

"Hi, Mrs. Williams."

"We need to talk. And not out here."

He showed her inside, and led her to the parlor decorated with an antique sofa flanked by two Queen Anne chairs. He'd jokingly called them Miss Ann's thrones.

He wasn't laughing now.

Ann was at the back of the house, working in the kitchen. He indicated for Donna to have a seat on the sofa.

She ignored the invitation. "Sydney called today."

What on earth? "That's nice. How is she doing?"

"She's coming home tomorrow."

His neck and face burned, as if someone had lit them on fire. "For a visit?"

"She's moving home. Permanently."

Coming here...to live? He staggered to a nearby chair and fell into it. Leaning his forearms on his knees, he hung his head as he tried to wrap his mind around what she was saying.

"She's finished rehab, and for the first time in a decade wants to move in with me. With family support, she really thinks she can make it this time."

"I see," he said to the floor.

"She says she looks forward to spending time with Hannah. And is excited to be well enough to have a relationship with her nieces and nephews."

Even though he wanted to scream his frustration at the timing, he felt a sense of release from the guilt. "Praise God," he said to this woman who had surely come to deliver the news as a blow.

"Well, you won't be praising God for long when you hear what else I have to say."

He looked up at Donna and found it difficult to believe someone as sweet as Hannah had been raised by this overbearing woman.

Donna's countenance fell, and for the first time, she appeared vulnerable. "I know I've been hard on you. And I know what I'm asking is even harder. But please...*please*...do the honorable thing this time."

He knew what she wanted before she had to ask. He saw the desperation in her eyes.

She touched his arm, but then snatched her hand away. "I know you love Hannah. I've watched you together. I've watched you with my grandchildren. They adore you. But they're young and will be fine.

"Sydney, on the other hand, is probably on her last hope. She's willing to come home and ask for help for the first time ever. We have to give her that."

He nodded, because even he had to acknowledge she spoke the truth.

"I need you to do the merciful thing and leave. I don't think Sydney can heal if she has to watch you and her own sister happy in love."

He forced himself to look into her eyes. All he'd wanted was to redeem himself, to have his father and Hannah—and now Donna—consider him an honorable man. So how could he risk hurting Sydney's recovery by staying?

He couldn't bear to destroy their family again. But how could he hurt Hannah by leaving?

If he stayed, he'd essentially be forcing Hannah to choose between him and Sydney. He couldn't put her in that position. And though Hannah wouldn't thank him for leaving, he knew with certainty that she would eventually understand.

"I can't make this decision without first discussing it with Hannah." Mark stood and walked out of the room and straight to his car. He couldn't even be polite enough to see her out. He had to do the hardest thing he'd ever done in his life.

Tell Hannah he needed to leave for good.

Chapter Thirteen

Hannah was as giddy as a teenager on her first date. She slipped into a sleek, sleeveless linen dress in ruby red, a color everyone always said was *her* color.

She smiled, knowing Anthony would be happy for her. During his battle with cancer, he'd told her over and over he wanted her to marry again. To find someone who would love her well. And love his children well.

She'd found that man.

After getting the little ones settled with Redd, she drove to Corinthia's finest restaurant, where Mark had told her to meet him.

The Iron Skillet, serving the best steak around, sat on the outskirts of town in a restored Victorian home. The steep prices kept her from eating there. But even if she could afford it, it wasn't a place for children.

She walked into the home with its luxurious carpet runner and grand staircase and was greeted by the maître d'. Mark had called to say he was on his way and had asked them to escort her to their table.

Her heart fluttered. If Mark was on his way, then he must have finished the conversation with Donna. Had it gone well?

Their table was actually in one of the private dining rooms upstairs. Proud of her calm facade, she stifled the urge to giggle like a fool over the royal treatment.

On their table, two dozen velvety red roses welcomed her. A red envelope propped beside the vase looked as if it could be a Valentine.

Surely not. Surely he hadn't remembered her whining about missing the romance of the day.

Tempted to open it, she touched the envelope, and nearly laughed when she fancied she heard it call her name. She flipped it over.

He'd written in rough scrawl, "Go ahead. You know you want to open it."

She did laugh out loud that time as she ripped open the envelope.

The card had a big pink heart on the front. A Valentine in June!

Her heart melted as it hit her that he *had* remembered. And he'd cared enough to give her roses and this sweet card that declared her his Valentine.

She couldn't imagine a better Valentine's Day. Until she heard him tell the maître d' they'd like privacy, then footsteps on the staircase.

Once again her heart fluttered. She sighed and smiled, waiting…

As soon as he walked in, she knew the meeting with Donna had not gone well.

She's won. Mom has won.

Hannah had no idea how she knew, but she did. Donna had changed his mind. "No," she said as he stopped beside the table. "You won't let her take this away from us."

He sat across from her and took hold of her hand. The look of devastation on his face nearly made her cry out.

She wanted to weep. This night was supposed to be perfect. And now…

"Happy Valentine's Day," he said. "I'm sorry I'm late."

"What happened?"

"I had this planned so perfectly. Every detail arranged. But—"

"You love me, or you wouldn't have gone to all this trouble." She squeezed his hand, willing her strength to infuse him. "You have to ignore Mom's ploys. She's seen us together now. She's probably desperate."

"Sydney's coming home tomorrow. To live."

Hannah's lungs squeezed shut. How could that

be? "But she hasn't lived in Corinthia since she was a teenager."

"Your mom said she's asked for family support and thinks she's going to be okay this time."

"She can't come here now. This isn't fair." *I should be happy for her. I know I should. What's wrong with me?*

"Your mom has asked me to leave." He ran his thumb over the top of Hannah's hand, the gesture so intimate, so comforting. Yet his words slashed at her heart.

Because she could tell he'd already made up his mind. "What did you tell her?"

"That I couldn't make that decision without talking to you."

He hadn't refused. Hadn't told Donna to mind her own business. He'd caved. He'd chosen Sydney and Sydney's welfare over her.

Once again, Sydney and her troubles trump everything.

How could Hannah have been so stupid to have believed Mark could put her above everyone else?

Mortified, her face tightened and burned. The mere thought of his betrayal made her want to throw her head on the table and wail. "You've already decided, haven't you? You're running again."

His brows drew together and he shook his head. "No. Not running. But I should go, to save you pain. I don't want you to feel like you have to choose between me and your sister."

She slid her hand out from under his and bound up her aching heart in the steel she needed to get through the next breath. "I'm tired of people deciding what's best for me."

Blood pulsed through her brain, throbbed in her temples. Sudden fury nearly blinded her, light flashing behind her eyes. Pushing back her chair, she stood and leaned forward, palms flat on the table. "My dad didn't consult me when he said it was best for the family if he left us. My sister didn't consult me when she decided to hang out with hoodlums and drink herself into oblivion."

She took a deep, shuddering breath. "My mom didn't consult me before she poured everything— including the house and my prom dress—into my sister's recovery. My husband didn't consult me before he decided it was best to scrimp on the life-insurance policy."

She leaned closer, too upset to cry. She would not embarrass herself. "And now you and Mom know what's best for me? For the Williams family?"

He stood and reached to touch her shoulder. "Hannah…"

She jerked away. Couldn't let him touch her. *Lord, help me. Help me walk out of here.* "Go back to Seattle. We were fine on our own when you got here. We'll be fine on our own after you leave."

He stared into her eyes, as if searching. "You're hurting right now. Please, sit down and let's talk about what's best for everyone involved."

She laughed, an ugly, sarcastic sound. "You don't get it. I'll be making my own decisions from here on out about what's best for me and my children. I've apparently made a mistake inviting you into our lives. But at least I found out now."

"I'm sorry." He stuffed his hands in his pockets, and tears filled his eyes.

How could his tears affect her, even after what he'd done? She squeezed her hands into fists to keep from reaching out to him. "I deserve a man who'd choose me over all others. God wants the best for me—someone who'll be by my side through the tough times. Now, I'd like for you to leave."

She couldn't look at him or surely she'd lose it. She turned away, only to stare directly at the vase full of roses. Her Valentine. He'd been thoughtful. But the items were simply things. Things he'd bought for her.

He hadn't been capable of giving her what she really needed after all.

She glanced over her shoulder and found him watching her. "Don't come back or it'll hurt the kids even more."

"Okay," he rasped.

Once his footsteps had faded down the stairs, she straightened herself and walked away. As she walked out, she nodded to the hostess, feeling overdressed and ridiculous for the hope she'd allowed herself not a half hour ago. She would not regret her decision to send him away. In some rational part of her brain, she knew she'd have to forgive him someday. It's what she'd been preaching all along. But at the moment, she just wanted to go home, climb into bed and cry.

The children were still awake when Hannah got home. They met her at the door with big grins.

She took a deep breath, forced a smile and said, "What's up?"

"You're early." Worry drew Redd's brows into an inverted V.

"Where's Mark?" Tony asked.

The simple question nearly brought her to her knees. "I'm not feeling well, so I came home."

Redd's eyes narrowed, and he probably saw too much. "Come on, kids, let's let your mom go to bed and rest." He gave her arm a squeeze. "I'll put them to bed."

"Thank you."

"But you have to find your surprises first!" Eric said.

"Yeah. We worked hard to hide them." Emily

tugged her hand. "Come on. Here's the first." She handed Hannah an envelope with Mark's writing on it.

Hannah's hands didn't want to move. She couldn't make sense of this game.

Emily grabbed the envelope and tore it open. She handed Hannah a homemade Valentine she felt sure Mark had had her children make. But in his handwriting, it said, "Your gift awaits. Follow the clues, starting with the twins' favorite spot to read."

With dread, she trudged to the chair Emily and Eric had sat in when Mark read to them. All four little ones followed right on her heels. Sure enough, slipped into the side of the cushion was another envelope.

As soon as she reached for it, the kids cheered, giggles filling the room.

She opened this one. Another kid-made card declared the next clue would be found in Tony's pet project. "Is it at the fence?" she asked. "Or would that be the rocking chairs?"

"The chairs," Tony said excitedly, as if he'd had his lips glued shut to try to keep from telling until now.

Outside they all went, Redd included. An envelope sat in the far rocker. This one told her she'd find her next clue with Blue's "food."

She tried to smile. The children were having so

much fun and had worked hard to keep the secret. She forced levity to her voice. "I wonder if that's in his bag of Purina or…" She tapped her chin. "Oh, I'll bet it's the bread cabinet!"

Squeals confirmed her guess.

That card said, "The last clue is hidden among Becca's favorite things."

The man knew her children well enough to know their favorite places and things.

But now he wouldn't be a part of their lives.

Pain gripped her insides as they went upstairs to Becca's bedroom. Hannah walked straight to the bookshelves, and in front of Becca's favorite book series sat a gift box.

Her hands shook as she opened it.

"Kids, why don't we let your mom open this in the privacy of her room?" Redd said.

"No, we want to see!" Becca said. "I've been good and kept the secret for ages!"

"It's okay," she told him as she opened the package. Inside lay a set of toy princess jewelry. A pair of dangly earrings and a huge pink-stoned, heart-shaped pendant.

Redd whistled.

"Do you like it, Mommy? We all picked it out!" Emily said.

"It's beautiful." She closed the box and, not wanting her kids to see her face, wrapped them in her arms. Their precious arms around her neck brought comfort. "Thank you all for helping Mark plan this surprise. He'll be so proud of you. Now, be good and let Mr. Redd tuck you in, okay?"

She kissed each one good-night and then dragged herself to her own room. She didn't want to explain anything to Redd. She just wanted to crawl under the covers and sleep.

But first she pulled out a stool and set the jewelry box on the highest shelf in her closet.

Mark had no idea when he bought a heart for her that he would be breaking one, as well.

Chapter Fourteen

As the first rays of sun peeked in the kitchen window, Mark fought the temptation to yank the curtains closed. The glow of the overhead lightbulb was about all the cheer he could take.

Sitting with Ann at the kitchen table, once again packed and ready to leave, he just needed to say a few goodbyes and be on his way.

He'd like to tell the Hughes children goodbye, but Hannah wouldn't allow it. He'd have to hope she made excuses for him.

He turned the coffee mug in his hands. "I'm sorry to keep you wondering if I'm staying or leaving. I'm really leaving this time."

"Oh, you're no bother at all. You're a busy man with obligations, and I'm sure it was difficult to get this time off."

A knock sounded on the back door. Then his

dad stuck his head inside. "I saw the lights on back here and figured you were up."

"Come in," Ann said. "I'll let you two talk." She poured Redd a cup of coffee and headed out of the kitchen.

"So…" his dad said as he stirred cream into the coffee "…figured you must be leaving town."

The two remained quiet as Mark continued spinning the cup, reading the slogan on each side: *Money can't buy love…but chocolate can.*

If only love were that easy.

"You wanna talk about what happened last night?" Redd asked, breaking the silence.

He'd figured his dad would notice. "Was she upset?"

"What do you think?"

Thinking of her pain twisted his gut in a knot that might never come out. "Donna asked me to do the honorable thing and leave because Sydney's coming home to stay."

Redd shook his head. "I don't know about that, son. Seems to me like it might be best for Sydney to deal with her past if she's ever going to get well."

"I told Hannah I can't take a chance on hindering her recovery."

"What does Hannah think?"

"She sent me packing."

Pursing his lips and scratching his head, Redd said, "Don't you think you should've worried about Hannah? About protecting *her?* She doesn't trust easily. Seems to me she's let you in her life and offered up her heart."

That offer was now off the table. Unable to sit still, he carried his mug to the sink. His dad's comment ate like acid on his nerves. "I'm sick about this. About how my past actions caused this whole situation. Now we're all suffering the consequences."

"Look how far you and I have come. There's still hope."

Not if Hannah had given up. He walked over to his dad and stuck out his hand to shake. "Time to go."

Instead of shaking, his dad stood. "Don't throw love away, son. I messed up with you. I don't want you to make the same mistakes."

He hadn't thrown it away. He'd simply tried to do what was right. "I'm not sure when I'll be back. Hannah thinks it'll be difficult for the children."

"Thanksgiving?"

"We'll see. Maybe instead, you can come out to Seattle to visit me."

Redd shook his head, disappointed.

"Hey, I'll fly you out, try to impress you with all my tools and 'toys' in the lab."

With a quick hug, Redd said, "You put Hannah first. We'll worry about the holiday later." Then he walked with Mark to his car.

Thunder rumbled in the distance as he drove away. A fitting send-off considering the way he felt inside.

The day was surreal. Hannah woke—for the second time—knowing Mark was gone. Even the atmosphere seemed oppressive, as if he'd sucked the oxygen out of Corinthia as he left. The skies had darkened, and another storm front was moving their way.

When she'd awakened earlier, she'd feared he might come see his dad to say goodbye. She hadn't dared look outside for his car. She'd pulled the covers over her head and hidden out, thankful Redd had called to offer to watch the kids for the day.

She stayed in bed as late as she could, allowing a short pity party. But then she forced her two feet to the floor and went back to life as usual.

Her heart felt bruised. Tender. *I miss him already.*

Rationally, she knew he would have left eventually anyway. Better she sent him on his way now. Before he could hurt her more.

Time for her to move on. Time to focus on her kids, her job and eventually building their dream house.

Time to deal with Sydney's return.

Strangely, her mother had called that morning, as well.

Who was she kidding? There was nothing strange about it. Donna had gotten her way, and now she wanted Hannah to be there when Sydney arrived to help ease the transition.

Hannah sighed numerous times as she showered and dressed for the day.

Just show Sydney you love her and support her, she kept reminding herself.

As Hannah opened the front door to leave, thunder rattled the window. She nearly screamed in fright, startled by a person standing there, soaking wet and about to ring the bell.

Though the woman's skin looked older than her thirty-two years, Hannah immediately recognized the brown eyes. "Sydney."

"Hi, sis."

The resentment fell away, and the joy of seeing her big sister lifted the heaviness of the day. "You look good." She wrapped her in a warm embrace.

Sydney was a little stiff, but then she melted into the hug and gave Hannah a tight squeeze in return. "I look and probably smell like that wet dog I just petted."

Lightning struck nearby, followed by an almost instantaneous boom. They both squealed. Then laughed.

"Come in out of the storm."

As they stepped inside the house, Sydney brushed wet hair off her forehead. "It's so good to see you, Hannah."

"I'm sorry I couldn't make the last family session. My job has been tough lately with the promotion, and I'm having some…trouble…with child care."

"That's okay. I totally understand." She smiled with bright, clear—sober—eyes. Nothing there but the old Sydney. And maybe a touch of sadness. "I hope you don't mind that I stopped by here first. Have to get my nerve up to face moving in with Mom."

A laugh escaped before Hannah could stop it. "I'm glad you came. Let's get you a towel." She led her sister to the kitchen and grabbed a large, fluffy bath towel out of the dryer. "Here you go. Let's sit at the table and visit awhile, then we'll go to Mom's together."

Their conversation started off slow like cold molasses, but eventually, they warmed to each other as they spoke about all that had been going on in their lives.

Of course, Hannah had to tiptoe around the past few weeks. She didn't mention Mark.

But one thought kept running through her head. *Would I have been forced to choose between them?* What if she were sitting here right now with Mark waiting in the background? Would it have changed the way she'd received her sister?

"You look great, Hannah. Are the kids here?"

Panic made her heart race. She didn't know how much Sydney was ready to handle. And wasn't sure how attached her kids might get to their aunt. "I—"

"It's okay. I understand if you want to wait a while before I see them."

"I'm sorry. I just don't know if it's good for them until I see whether you're going to stay. They've...well, they've lost a lot." *And will have another loss today when they find out Mark's gone.*

"Totally understandable." She gave Hannah's hand a squeeze and smiled to encourage her.

A generous gesture that put Hannah to shame. "They're not here right now anyway. Redd Ryker offered to watch them for me today."

"Wow, I never would have guessed Mom would let her grandkids hang out with a Ryker."

Tension gripped the muscles across Hannah's neck and shoulders. "You guessed correctly. I've been working on her, though. Trying to get her to forgive Mar— Sorry."

"You can say his name. I've worked through our issues."

Should I bring it up? She stared into Sydney's clear brown eyes and debated.

"What is it, Hannah?"

She couldn't wait. Couldn't start out with a lie between them. "He's been home. Mark came home."

"Really?" Her expression brightened. "I'm glad. For him. And for his dad."

Oh, Lord, this could be so damaging to Sydney. Please help her. "And for you? Were you hoping to see him?"

"Actually, no. But I'd welcome the chance to talk."

She felt as if her heart was going to beat right out of her chest. "To give him a piece of your mind?"

Sydney was taken aback. "Goodness, no. I'm well beyond hating Mark. As much as Mom has tried to keep me holding on to a grudge, my counselor has helped me work through what happened. Besides, he didn't force me to do anything."

She grabbed her sister's hand and wanted to sob with relief. "So you're really better this time."

"I am. I've blamed everyone else—even Mom—for all the bad decisions I made. Mark wasn't to blame in the first place."

"Do you still have feelings for him?"

Sydney laughed. "Of course not. What's with the focus on Mark, Hannah?"

Like a dam with gallons and gallons of water backed up, words pushed against her lips, and guilt boosted the power. "I love him" burst out along with a gush of tears and big, heaving sobs. She tried to wipe the tears away to see her sister. Dreading Sydney's reaction.

Sydney's eyes widened. But then Hannah couldn't see through the tears. She swiped at her eyes with her sleeve. "Sydney?"

Her sister grabbed her into a big hug. "Oh, Hannah, it's okay."

She stood in her sister's arms and cried all the tears she'd held back over the past twelve hours. "And now he's gone. I sent him away."

"Oh, sweetie." Sydney comforted her, rubbing her back, smoothing her hair off her face.

"I thought you would hate me. But I was ready to give up everything for him—you, Mom… I'm so selfish. I wanted him to love me enough to put me first." She sniffed and grabbed a tissue. "Yet he listened to Mom and chose to protect you."

"That's not right. I'm okay with you and Mark. Sure, I have a lot of stuff to work through. But nothing to do with him."

After wiping her eyes and blowing her nose, she took Sydney's hand and led her back to the table. "I'm sorry. I sound like a spoiled baby."

"No, you have every right to be angry. My problems robbed you of so much." She gripped Hannah's hands and blinked away her own tears. "Over the last few months, I've had to come to terms with all the devastation my addictions have caused. And I'm sorry. I hope you'll forgive me."

Hannah couldn't believe they were having this conversation. She'd worried about hurting Sydney, yet had felt guilty about not caring enough for her sister to resist loving Mark. While the whole time, Sydney was dealing with her own guilt. "Of course I forgive you. I love you, and I'm glad you're home."

She truly meant it. Forgiving Sydney eased a burden she'd been carrying, and the weight of many years began to lift.

"Thank you. Now, tell me everything about Mark. Surely we can work it out." She gave a little laugh. "Believe me, I'm the queen of working out problems."

Chapter Fifteen

Mark stared at the screen on the headrest of the seat in front of him. His flight had been delayed hours due to heavy rains and wind. Now they were finally in the air on what seemed an endless journey toward Seattle. *Home.*

The problem was, he'd started to think of Corinthia as home.

He touched the screen to view the map, to see how much farther they had to go. The map showed their progress along the route with a line that led all the way back to Atlanta. As the little picture of the plane moved farther and farther away from Georgia, he felt sick in his gut. A physical pain, as if he were being pulled away from Hannah and the children like a rubber band about to snap, breaking some sort of connection. He couldn't stand watching the miles pile up between them.

But she'd made her choice. He knew, in the long run, it would be best.

Donna would have never accepted him anyway.

He leaned his head back and closed his eyes.

God, show me Your will. Your way. Help me to accept Your plans for my life.

The plane inched farther away from Hannah, and Mark wanted to make it stop. But he had to resist the temptation to return to her.

She no longer wanted him.

And, ultimately, hadn't he done what he thought honorable and right by honoring Donna's wishes?

He turned the screen to a movie channel, but the film faded as he closed his eyes and wished for sleep.

Hannah wrapped her arm around her sister's waist, offering strength. She nodded toward their mom's back door.

Sydney opened it and stepped inside. "Hi, Mama."

Donna whipped her head around from the pot she was stirring. "Well, whataya know. My girls." She gave them a wobbly smile with tears in her eyes. Then she wrapped them in her arms. "Welcome home."

Though Hannah knew she was talking to Sydney, she had a sense that maybe her mom was welcoming her, as well. But that caused mixed feelings. She was still angry with her mother, yet relieved some part of their disagreement was over.

After they unloaded Sydney's luggage and a few boxes of belongings from the car, they gathered around the table.

Hannah had a plan she hoped might help them deal with the past—as a family. She hoped to get her mother to open up and talk so maybe, just maybe, she could let it all go.

"Mom, I see you're cooking," Hannah said. "But I was really hoping you and Sydney could come out to my house for dinner tonight. So you can both spend some time with the kids."

A tense, closemouthed smile stretched the skin on Donna's face. "You're welcome to eat here with us. I would love to see them."

Sydney leaned forward on her arms, looking relaxed, and offered a genuine smile. "I'd really like to go out there, have an official tour. Seven people around this table would be a little crowded."

"It seats eight if we squeeze in." Donna looked back and forth between them. "What are you two up to?"

Sydney nodded at Hannah to encourage her.

Hannah took a deep breath and willed her heart rate to slow. "Sydney and I have talked. I told her everything."

Donna's thunderous expression put the recent

storm to shame. "Hannah, you didn't." She reached across the table to Sydney. "Honey, are you okay?"

"I'm fine, Mama. I forgave Mark a long time ago. And after working through my problems with a counselor, I came to realize he wasn't at fault."

"But he introduced you to that bad crowd. Bought you alcohol."

"And he also tried to keep me away from it as soon as he saw I had a problem. But I wouldn't listen. I began hanging around those kids by myself." She grabbed both her mother's hands and squeezed, her knuckles turning white. "Mama, I did it for attention. To be accepted."

"That's silly. You had plenty of attention. You were popular at school. Had straight As. Teachers loved you. You were president of the sophomore class. You—"

"I was unhappy."

Donna shook her head in disbelief. "What? We gave you everything."

"You and Daddy weren't getting along. I overheard him talking to you about divorce." Sydney's nostrils flared. "I heard him snoring on the couch each night. Heard you crying in the bedroom."

Donna's hand patted and plucked at the neckline of her shirt as her face went colorless. "Your daddy failed us. He took away everything. Just like Mark did. Men can't be trusted. I had to protect you. Both of you."

Silence stilled the air, the tick-tick of the wall clock the only thing registering the passage of time as their mother's eyes darted back and forth between them.

Donna dragged her attention away from her eldest daughter to Hannah, worry still etched on her face. "Don't you understand why I had to protect you from Mark?"

Hannah struggled to take a deep breath and prayed for wisdom. "It's time to let go of the past. If Sydney's let it go, and I've let it go, then you need to, as well. And not just for Mark's sake or even Dad's sake. We need to do this for our sake—the sake of our family."

Donna jumped up, bumping the edge of the table, sending it scraping a couple of inches across the floor. "How can you two act like nothing ever happened? I've always had to protect you girls. I'll do it even if you hate me for it." She ran from the room, but not before a whimper escaped from her throat.

Hannah's eyes stung with tears as she looked at Sydney. "Thank you."

"I didn't want to hurt her. But we all need to face the truth or we'll never get better."

Hannah stood and reached out her hand. "Come on, Aunt Sydney. Let's go spend some time with the kids."

Chapter Sixteen

Early Monday morning, Mark dragged himself to his office. Something he usually found fulfilling, a joy, had become a chore. All his employees smiled and welcomed him back, but he missed Hannah. Missed her children. Missed his dad.

He walked into his spacious, plush office devoid of anything personal, other than design drawings he'd done in college and three framed diplomas. Sat in his cushy leather chair and spread work on his outrageously expensive desk. All the trappings of success.

He tried to drown himself in the backlog of work, but his mind wandered. He couldn't focus. What was he working for?

His goal had been to achieve success so his life wouldn't be a waste. So maybe one day he could go home and show everyone he'd made something of himself. That he wasn't a loser.

But God had already shown him he was valuable in His sight. Why did he stay on the treadmill to earn more and more when he had more than he'd need for one lifetime?

Besides, what was money and success if he didn't have someone to share it with? If he didn't have someone to love him?

Ann's coffee-cup slogan popped into his mind and made him laugh. *Money can't buy love.* Maybe God had been trying to show him something even then.

And hadn't God proven the point the whole time he was in Corinthia? No matter what he tried to *do* for people—with money—his efforts hadn't made a difference.

But when he spent time working with them, relationships had started to slowly improve. What if he went back and *showed* them he wanted to commit to them? Showed Donna he was committed to Hannah.

Showed *Hannah* he was committed to Hannah.

But hadn't he done that already?

His assistant, with her curly blond hair and typical navy blue suit, tapped on his door as she stepped into his office. "Here's that file you asked for." She smiled as she set it on his desk.

"I'm about to schedule these appointments you called about." She closed the door as she left.

But had he really showed Hannah? He pulled out his cell phone to look at a photo he'd snapped of Hannah playing with her kids.

Hannah. He wanted to call. To see how she was doing.

But she'd sent him away.

He'd thought leaving was the right thing to do. Yet how had his leaving, even at her request, made Hannah feel?

He ran his hand over his jaw and grimaced. He'd tried his best not to think about it. Not to face the fact of how it would hurt her. But now in Seattle, away from Donna's threats, he had to face the truth. He hadn't shown Hannah he wanted to commit at all.

Hannah would feel as if he'd chosen Sydney over her. Just like her own mother always had. The very worst thing he could have done. *Oh, Lord, help me make it up to her.*

Thinking of her pain—pain he'd caused—knifed at his heart.

He had to go back. *Go home.* His true home was in Corinthia with Hannah.

He buzzed his assistant. He'd have her set up those meetings in Atlanta. If they wanted his company, they could meet him there sometime that week.

Because he was going to take the first flight back.

No matter how bad things looked with Hannah and her family, he had to return and fight for her. She needed someone to choose *her*.

He wouldn't quit until he had Donna's blessing. Sydney's blessing. And Hannah's, too.

Within two hours, he'd made all arrangements and rushed to the airport without even going home to grab clothes. He ran to the gate and barely boarded in time. Grateful for good weather, he collapsed into his seat.

The flight took off without a hitch. This time, as the little plane on the screen inched toward Atlanta, his heartbeat seemed erratic. He couldn't remember ever being so anxious.

She could reject him outright.

Hope and fear battled as the plane landed several hours later.

Wanting to surprise her, he picked up a rental car and made a reservation at the Gunters' B and B, making Mrs. Gunter promise to tell no one. He planned to go to the bank to see Hannah first thing the next morning.

He prayed it wasn't a dumb plan. She'd be surprised, that was for sure. And maybe not too happy with him. But at least he wouldn't make her truly angry by showing up when the kids were around, because he knew she'd be protective of them.

His job now was to convince her he loved her.

That he wasn't going to leave her again. And that he wouldn't give up trying to win over her family.

Lord, I'm going home again. From the beginning, I've felt You leading me there. I pray it's not my selfish desires. And that Hannah will accept me.

He put on his left blinker as he merged onto the interstate and pointed the car toward home.

Hannah sat at her desk, going through the motions of work. So much had changed in three days. Including her feelings for Mark. Well, the *feelings* hadn't changed so quickly as the hope for possibilities.

She drummed her fingers on the desk, trying her best not to pick up her cell phone. The compulsion to check for a message or missed call had pulled her from her work numerous times already that morning.

Enough was enough.

She tossed the phone into her purse and yanked out her keyboard. Determined to do her very best as branch manager, she wheeled closer to her desk and opened a file folder.

A familiar voiced drifted back to her from the lobby area.

I'm losing it. Even hearing his voice.

Defeated, she slapped the folder closed. "Get a grip, Hannah."

"Talking to yourself now, are you?"

Every molecule in the universe, every atom in her body, zeroed in on the doorway and the man standing there.

She blinked. With no sunglasses this time, his golden gaze seemed to soak her in as he looked from her lips to her eyes. And back again.

No words. She had no words.

Then suddenly, her senses returned, and her brain caught up to her racing heart. "Did you stay in Georgia?"

"No. I've been to Seattle and back." His wrinkled white oxford shirt and creased khaki slacks gave testament to his cross-country travel.

She couldn't read his expression and remained seated, her heart pounding slow and hard. "Why'd you come back?"

"I was wrong to leave."

Hope gave wings to her soul. "I sent you away."

"Yes, you did. But I still shouldn't have gone." His tired eyes shone bright. Passionate. "I didn't consider your feelings like I should have. I've been stupid. Blinded by my pride—wanting to gain respect."

"So, what are you saying?"

"I'm saying I love you."

A gasp sounded out in the hallway. An eavesdropping coworker.

For the first time, Mark allowed an inkling of a smile. Then he closed the door and walked around the end of her desk. He pulled her to her feet, but let go of her hands. "I'm here to fight for you. To battle until your mom and Sydney have forgiven me. Until you learn to trust me again."

Words she'd longed to hear. But could she believe them? "You hurt me. Hurt the kids. They've been moping around the house for days." She didn't need to inform him she had been, too. "Why this sudden change?"

"When I went to the office yesterday, I realized all I've worked for pales in comparison to loving you and spending time with you." He lifted her chin and looked into her eyes, his own filled with love. And worry. "I've been moping, too. I'm sorry I left when I should have loved you first and foremost and trusted God to work out the rest."

Happiness seemed within her grasp. But one barrier remained. "How could a relationship possibly work cross-country?"

"I'm selling my company. Moving here permanently."

Chills ran along her face, neck and down her arms, and she burst into tears.

He pulled her into his arms. "It's okay. Somehow, we'll get through to your family. We'll do this together."

"Oh, Mark. God's been working already." She wrapped her arms around his waist and let him comfort her as she cried until tears soaked his shirtfront.

He patiently rubbed her back, smoothed her hair and waited until she'd stopped with the worst of the sobs. "How's it been going with Sydney?"

"You won't believe it."

He pulled two chairs together for them to talk. "Try me."

"Sydney is doing so well. She's almost like her old self. And—" she gripped his arm "—she doesn't blame you."

He leaned back in his chair and whistled. "Wow. God really has been at work."

Her heart sang, and joy bubbled out in a care-free laugh as she anticipated him experiencing release from guilt. She would give him and Sydney the chance to talk. Would invite him and Redd to dinner.

But what about her mom?

She'd invite her, as well. It couldn't hurt, could it?

A dozen scenarios, none of them good, flashed though Mark's mind as he drove along the light-dappled driveway through the tunnel of trees that had so often brought him a sense of peace.

The only peace he had at the moment was Hannah's declaration that God had been working.

That could only be a good thing.

He'd been to the hardware store and had spent the afternoon with his dad. Had been explaining his plans on their way to Hannah's for dinner. But his dad had been suspiciously quiet.

"So, do you have any idea what's been going on with Hannah and her family?" Mark asked.

"You've already asked me that. Told you I'd let her fill you in."

He chuckled. "Thought I might catch you off guard. I'd really like to know what I'm walking into."

Redd gestured toward the house. "Is her family going to be here?"

"I assumed Sydney would be."

He thought his dad smiled but couldn't be sure. As they parked and walked over to the house, Redd looked like a man heading to his own funeral.

Great. This might not go well.

The front door opened, and all four kids came streaming out. They tackled Mark at the bottom of the steps, an enthusiastic welcome he didn't deserve.

A lump the size of a boulder clogged his throat,

so instead of speaking, he knelt down to hug each one.

"I knew you'd come back," Tony said as he pressed into Mark's side.

Emily, who'd thrown herself into his arms, nuzzled his neck. "I missed you. Will you read to me tonight?"

He tweaked her nose. "Well, that'll depend on your mom's plans. We can ask her if you want."

All business, Becca pushed up her glasses as she nodded. "Yes, let's ask."

Steps sounded on the porch. And then there she was. Hannah. She stood watching, tears in her eyes. Her raven hair shone in the evening sun. A swirly skirt skimmed her shins, and a sleeveless emerald sweater highlighted her creamy skin and matching eyes.

The pink princess necklace he'd given her glinted in the sunlight.

When he looked from the necklace into her eyes, she touched the pendant and smiled.

"Where'd you go?" Eric asked.

"I had to go back to Seattle to take care of some business," he said to Eric. Then he looked back up to Hannah. "But I'm home now."

Tony inched his way closer and rested his arm across Mark's shoulder. "Home? I thought Seattle was your home."

Becca flicked a piece of grass off his knee.

Emily wiggled, her hair brushing his chin. Eric elbowed his twin, trying to move in closer.

Having four children glued to him felt more like home than anything in Seattle ever had. He smiled up at Hannah. "From now on, Corinthia will be my home."

The kids' celebration knocked him off balance, and he landed in the grass with the four of them piled on top of him. Laughter and giggles warmed him from his heels to his grassy hair. Their unconditional acceptance was a real live demonstration of God's grace in his life.

If only Hannah's mother and sister would welcome him with one fraction of that acceptance.

Hannah reached out and helped Tony up. "Come on, kids. Mark's had a long day. Dinner will be ready soon."

Redd helped peel children off Mark, taking the twins' hands and leading them inside. Mark put his arm around Becca and ruffled Tony's hair as he and Hannah headed toward the kitchen.

"Come on, young'uns, let's go wash up." Redd herded the four to the powder room.

A delicious-smelling pot of spaghetti sauce simmered on the stove as he and Hannah walked in.

"My standby," she said.

"I love spaghetti. Would never get tired of it."

The blush on her cheeks deepened as she pushed hair behind her ears, telling him the compliment had pleased her. She lifted the lid and stirred the sauce.

He couldn't resist brushing his hand over the smooth, blushing skin as he tilted her head his direction. "Thank you for having me here. For letting me see your children. I promise I'll try my best not to hurt them again."

She rested her cheek in his hand and closed her eyes. "I know you won't."

When she opened her emerald-green eyes and looked into his, he knew he wanted to be right here, with her, for the rest of his life. All the background noise faded. Nothing existed but the two of them in that moment. "I love you more than anything," he whispered.

She cupped his jaw, ran her thumb over his bottom lip. "I love you, too. And I—"

The doorbell rang. He groaned in response.

She smiled, stood on her tiptoes and gave him a quick kiss.

Lightning jolted through his body in response. "Is that Sydney at the door?"

She looked away then directly at him, uncertainty in her eyes. Her hands fluttered nervously to the neck of her sweater; then she grabbed the pendant and zipped it along the chain. "Sydney... and, I'm hoping, my mother."

So she had invited them both. He found her anxiety alarming. And actually worried more about seeing Donna than Sydney. He did not want some kind of showdown in front of the kids.

"Should the children be here?"

She took hold of his hand and held tightly as they walked out of the kitchen. "I have a feeling it'll be okay."

A feeling? Was that enough?

The doorbell rang again.

"Hey, kids," Mark called as they passed the hand-washing commotion. "How about going out back and feeding Blue his dinner? Do you know how to?"

Becca's eyes lit up. "Sure do." She didn't hesitate a moment but raced toward the back door. The others followed.

"So much for their clean hands," Redd said. "You gonna answer that door sometime today?"

Mark looked at Hannah and raised his brows. "Let's do this."

When they opened the front door, Donna and Sydney stood side by side on the porch, although Donna faced slightly sideways.

As if she couldn't bear to look at him.

His gut hit his feet. But he couldn't worry about Donna right now. He smiled at Sydney, whose eyes seemed bright and clear. "Wow, you look great."

When he reached out to shake her hand, she ignored his hand and hugged him. "I'd say the same about you. You've grown up."

"Come in, you two," Hannah said.

As Donna walked by him, he said, "Hello, Mrs. Williams."

"Mark." She nodded a greeting and continued her march inside.

Redd stepped into the room. "Hannah, can I help — Oh, hello, ladies."

Donna held her purse in front of her in both hands like a shield. She nodded stiffly to him. "Thank you for babysitting the last couple of days. But I'd like to see my grandkids now."

His brow furrowed. His eyes darted to Hannah. Then to Sydney. When he looked at her, his expression softened. "Welcome home, Sydney."

"Thank you, Mr. Ryker. I'm doing really well."

"Redd, call me Redd." He gave her a pat on the shoulder.

Then he stepped into Donna's space. "Let's make one thing clear. I've gotten attached to those kids, so if you're back in the picture, you better be willing to share."

Donna's face reddened. Flummoxed, her mouth flapped open and closed.

"Of course she will, won't you, Mom?" Hannah said, stifling a laugh, but failing and letting go with a grin.

The thought of his dad loving those kids like Mark did...

Mark hoped he could be their stepdad. That Redd could be a step-grandfather for Hannah's children.

Finally, Donna's mouth snapped shut, and she turned and stalked toward the kitchen. Redd followed, as if making sure she wouldn't abscond with his "grandkids."

Mark nodded toward Donna. "Well, that didn't go well."

"Don't mind Mama. She's trying," Sydney said. "So...Hannah tells me you two have feelings for each other."

His gaze jerked to Hannah, who smiled encouragement.

"Um, yes."

"I'm happy for you both." Her eyes were clear, and she did truly look happy.

Surreal. The moment he'd worried about for years, and Sydney ended up being kind, generous. "Thank you. That means a lot to me. I hope you can forgive me for what I did in high school."

"I don't blame you for any of my past mistakes. We were both young and naive. You were hurting. I was hurting...and stupid." She shrugged. "And now life goes on. You two deserve to be happy."

"Thank you." Once again, Mark couldn't believe God's generosity. Should never have doubted His power—His healing power.

Hannah took Mark's hand. "Come on. Let's go check on dinner."

He had to laugh. "No basking in forgiveness, huh? I have to once again face your mother."

Hannah and Sydney put their arms around each other and gave him a look of sympathy. Then they laughed.

Seeing the two of them relaxed together brought a sense of relief…and contentment.

When they reached the kitchen, they found Redd at the table telling Donna how much he enjoyed her chocolate pound cakes.

"Well, uh, Redd, I'll give you the recipe if you like."

No more *those Rykers?*

Redd waved off the offer. "Nah, I'm sure I'd never make it as tasty as yours."

Donna seemed pleased. If he didn't know better, he'd think his dad was flirting. Why, Donna was even blushing. But then she spotted Mark.

Her smile fled fast as a fifty-knot wind. She turned to the stove and took up stirring the sauce with one hand while adjusting a knob on the stove top with the other. Steam rose off a pot of boiling water. "Hannah, the noodles are almost ready."

"Thanks, Mom. I'll call the kids to come in and wash up."

"Wait," Donna said. She bowed her head and braced her hands against the oven handle.

Was she praying?

Drawing in a deep breath, she lifted her head. "Mark, I need to apologize."

"Excuse me?" He didn't know what he'd expected. But it wasn't that.

"I've been stubborn...have refused to let go of hurts from the past." It seemed she had to drag the words out, each one painful. "But the last couple of days, my daughters have been examples of forgiving and moving on. I'm ashamed of how I've let pain from my past hurt my girls when all I ever wanted was to protect them."

With tears in her eyes, she looked lovingly at Hannah...then at Sydney. "They've been good role models for their ol' mom."

Hannah and Sydney embraced their mom. But she quickly broke away.

Facing Mark fully, Donna raised her chin. "Mark Ryker, I forgive you. Will you forgive me?"

Mark thought he might need to sit down. But instead, he walked over to her—this woman who'd been so spiteful and hard. A woman now asking for his forgiveness.

Only God could have done that.

He gripped both her hands. "Thank you. Of course I forgive you."

For a second, he thought she might hug him.

But then she seemed to think better of it and gave her head a firm nod. "Thank you. Now, Hannah, go get my grandbabies."

When she turned back to the pot of sauce, he looked over at his dad. Misty-eyed and grinning, Redd yanked his head toward Hannah, who was going out the back door. "I think maybe you two need a moment alone together. Send the young'uns inside. I think Tony owes his nana a tour of his bedroom."

Before going out the door, Mark stopped by the stove. "Mrs. Williams."

"Call me Donna." She didn't look at him, but kept stirring and fiddling with the garlic bread.

"I'd like your blessing to ask Hannah to marry me."

All her fluttery movement stopped. The whole kitchen stilled, except for the bubbling, boiling water. It seemed the whole room held its breath.

"Do you love her?"

"Yes, ma'am, very much. I'll treasure her every day of my life."

"She loves you. I can tell. And I know my grandkids love you."

"I love them, too. I'll do everything to watch over them, to take care of them like their own dad would want."

She looked him in the eye, assessing him. He hoped he measured up.

"Do you plan to move back home to Corinthia? To make your place in this community? And in our church?"

"Yes. I've found this is where I belong."

With a firm nod, she said, "Okay, then. I give you my blessing."

A smile stole across his face. And then across hers. Before he knew it, he grabbed her for a big hug. "Thank you." He released her and hurried to the door. "If you'll excuse me, I have some proposing to do."

Hannah nearly floated across the backyard. Her family was well on the way to healing. She felt whole for the first time in…well, in over a decade.

She tried but couldn't pull her children away from Blue. They loved the dog like a member of the family, wanted to wait for him to finish eating so they could reward him with a doggie biscuit.

"Your nana says to come and eat," Mark called as he joined them behind the house.

They took off like little arrows shot all at once from a bow.

"Now, why wouldn't they do that for me? I've been out here trying to pull them away from Blue, but they wouldn't budge."

"I guess I just have the touch." He bumped her shoulder and gave a goofy wiggle of his eyebrows.

"That's simply not fair."

He put his hands around her waist and pulled her close. "I'll tell you what wouldn't be fair."

"What?" She snuggled in, enjoying how perfectly she fit.

"If you wouldn't say yes to marrying me."

She sucked in a breath, scared to move. Scared he would laugh. Was he kidding, or did he really mean what she thought he meant? "So...is that a joke, or a proposal in an awful, unromantic, roundabout way?"

Red streaked across his cheeks. "Sorry. I'm new at this. Meant to do a better job." He fell to one knee and took her hands into his. He looked nervous until he smiled. A smile that left her knees quivering.

"Hannah Lyn Williams Hughes, I love you with all my heart. I love your children, too. I want to raise Becca, Tony, Eric and Emily, to be a father to them." His voice cracked.

When she started to speak, he held up his hand to stop her.

He cleared his throat. "I've received the blessing of your mother and would very much love for you to do me the honor of marrying me. If you'll have me with all my faults and failings."

Tears stung behind her nose and eyes. "You asked her?"

"Yes, I did. And she grilled me something good."

Hannah could only imagine. "She gave her blessing?"

He nodded, his golden eyes earnest. He looked scared, as if she could possibly refuse him.

God, thank You. Only through Your power...
"Yes. Yes!" She pulled him to his feet.

"I'll build you that house you want. Just as soon as we find a good piece of property. I promise."

She shook her head, and for a moment, she couldn't find her voice. All she'd wanted, thought she needed, paled in comparison to the man standing in front of her, declaring his love. "It doesn't matter. We could be happy here. Even invite your dad to move in with us."

"But it's been your dream. To have an idyllic place of your own."

"I don't need it now. I have you. Anyplace is home if it's filled with your love."

He kissed her then in this perfect moment, this perfect place. And the kiss promised all the love and security she would ever need.

* * * * *

Dear Reader,

Thank you so much for once again spending time in my fictional town of Corinthia, Georgia! I hope you enjoyed revisiting Gabe and Faith from the previous story, *A Family for Faith*. It was fun to see Hannah, a secondary character from that book, have a shot at true love and happiness in her own story. I think Mark was the perfect match.

Of course, the journey wasn't easy! Hannah and Mark had to learn that they couldn't buy security and acceptance. Both came from God alone. If you're looking for love and security, I hope you'll look toward God, who loves you beyond your wildest imagination, who offers the ultimate in security.

Thank you so much for reading my book! I love hearing from readers. Please tell me what you think about *A House Full of Hope*. You can visit my website, www.missytippens.com, or email me at missytippens@aol.com. If you don't have internet access, you can write to me c/o Love Inspired Books, 233 Broadway, Suite 1001, New York, NY 10279.

Missy Tippens

Questions For Discussion

1. In *A House Full of Hope,* Mark is the bad boy who has come home seeking redemption. How would you feel if you were his father?

2. How would you feel if you were Mark, and your dad (or another family member) reacted like Redd did?

3. Early in the story, the reader learns Hannah has been holding on to a lot of anger since childhood. How could Hannah have handled it differently?

4. Mark wanted to achieve success before returning home so he'd earn respect. What pitfalls do you see in striving for material success? Have you ever fallen into that same trap?

5. What does Jesus have to say about earthly belongings in the Bible?

6. What do you think is the theme of the story?

7. What in Mark's past made it difficult for him to stay and fight for Hannah when he learned Sydney was coming home?

8. Hannah longed for security. Why? What, in your life, gives you security and how would it affect you if your security was taken away?

9. Hannah and her mother struggled to see eye to eye when it came to Mark. Do you think Hannah was right in pursuing a relationship with him against her mother's wishes? When getting involved in a relationship, have you ever gone against someone's advice?

10. How did you feel about Hannah striving to own a home? Do you have something you long for and work toward like she did?

11. Discuss the two Bible verses listed in the beginning of the book, 1 Corinthians 13:13 and Ephesians 2:4–5. How do they relate to the story? How do they relate to your life?

12. Mark learned his love of creating and building from his father's workshop at the store. What loves have you inherited from your parents or role models? Did those loves affect your career choices?

13. Mark felt guilt over his brother's death. Have you experienced guilt in a relationship? Or have you been on the other end, the one who's been wronged? Would an apology help repair the relationship?

LARGER-PRINT BOOKS!

GET 2 FREE
LARGER-PRINT NOVELS
PLUS 2 FREE
MYSTERY GIFTS

Love Inspired

Larger-print novels are now available...

LILPI 18